Alan W. Livingston has had a unique history in the entertainment business, having been President and later Chairman of the Board of Capitol Records, Inc., Vice President in Charge of Television Programming for NBC, and Senior Vice President and President of the Entertainment Group of Twentieth Century-Fox Film corporation. At Capitol, in charge of all creative operations, Livingston's personal input involved everything from his creation of Bozo the Clown to the signing of Frank Sinatra. He created the famous Capitol children's library, writing and producing "Sparky's Magic Piano," "Rusty in Orchestraville," and recordings featuring Bugs Bunny, Woody Woodpecker, Walt Disney characters and others. For the teenage market, he signed such artists as the Beach Boys and the Beatles, and brought the latter to the United States. At NBC, he was directly responsible for "Bonanza", one of the most successful series in the company's history. "Ronnie Finkelhof, Superstar" is Livingston's first novel. He lives in Beverly Hills with his wife, actress Nancy Olson.

RONNIE FINKELHOF, SUPERSTAR

Alan W. Livingston

FAWCETT JUNIPER • NEW YORK

RLI: $\dfrac{\text{VL 6 \& up}}{\text{IL 7 \& up}}$

A Fawcett Juniper Book
Published by Ballantine Books
Copyright © 1988 by Alan W. Livingston

Library of Congress Catalog Card Number: 87-47830

ISBN 0-449-70134-4

Manufactured in the United States of America

First Edition: March 1988

CHAPTER

1

Ronnie and I had just come through the food line at the school cafeteria and were carrying loaded trays, looking for a place to sit. It was lunchtime, and the place was jammed. Ronnie was ahead of me, and as we passed a table with two girls and two guys at it, I overheard one of them say, "There goes Finkel-schmuck." Then the other guy said, "With his friend Sambo." I always figure later what I should have done—in hindsight when it's too late. I should have said, "My *friend's* name is *Finkelhof*, and *my* name is *Sam*, not *Sambo*," and then I ought to have dumped my tray of food right on top of their honky heads. But when you're black, you're conditioned to count to ten. I should have counted to about one and a half! The girls were giggling, but I just kept on walking. I was glad Ronnie didn't hear it.

While we were eating, I noticed that Ronnie kept looking over at that table. I thought maybe he did hear them after all. But he did not look upset or anything, so I kept my mouth shut. Then, just as we were finishing, this girl came up to our table. She was one of the ones that thought her boyfriend's remarks were so funny.

"Hi, Ronnie," she said. She was some good-looking chick, I have to say that for her—blond, blue-eyed, with a figure like you dream about. She was wearing blue jeans so tight that they were pulled right up into her crotch so that you could see the outline of everything. I always wondered about that—if it was uncomfortable. You know what I mean. The T-shirt she was wearing was also having trouble holding her in.

Ronnie jumped up so fast he almost knocked over the table. "Hi, Ginny," he kind of stammered.

Ginny didn't look at me—like I wasn't even there—so I didn't bother to get up. Not that I would have anyway. "Can I borrow a couple of quarters for the Coke machine?" she said. "We're all out at my table." Ginny had her motor running while she was standing there, and I wondered why in hell she was putting on the sexy act for Finkelhof. I glanced over at her table, and got the picture very fast. They were looking our way, watching the whole scene as if "Finkelschmuck" might give them some entertainment. Ronnie *is* kind of a nerd, and unfortunately he didn't let them down.

"Sure, Ginny," he said as he fumbled in his pockets for change. Finally he found two quarters, but the poor goof was so nervous that he dropped one of them in his glass of milk. Ronnie looked down at the glass. Then he fumbled some more, but he had no more quarters. Neither did I, or I would have come to the rescue. Ginny just stood there smiling like nothing was wrong. Finally Ronnie handed her the one quarter he still had in his hand. Ginny still just stood there, waiting. Why didn't Ron just tell her to get lost?

Ronnie looked back at the glass of milk. Finally he picked it up, drank the whole thing down in a gulp, and retrieved the quarter from his mouth. Then he wiped it off on his napkin, and sort of hesitatingly handed it to Ginny. She took it like it was all perfectly natural, said, "Thanks, Ronnie, you're a doll," and sashayed back to her group, wiggling her body all the way. I don't think Ronnie even noticed the giggling at her table. He just stood there looking after her with his mouth hanging open. He didn't get it.

"Sit down, Ron," I said. He still just stood there. "Hey, sit down, man." I tugged at his sleeve. "Better yet, let's get out of here."

"I haven't finished my lunch," Ronnie said as he finally sat down. He still didn't get it.

"You dig that chick?" Ronnie just stared at his plate. "Hey, man, we're friends," I said. "You can tell me."

"What if I do? Most of the time she doesn't even say hello to me. Besides, she's goin' with Andy Hamilton, Big Man on Campus. Even if she were friendly, I wouldn't know what to say to her." Ronnie still had his head in his plate—he wasn't too comfortable when it came to the opposite sex.

"Hey . . . you a virgin?" I always wondered about that, and figured it was about time I found out.

"Are *you*?" Ronnie asked.

"Hell, no!"

Ronnie was quiet, and went back to eating. Finally he looked up. "Sam . . . ?"

"Yeah?"

"I guess I can tell you."

"What?" I figured this conversation might get some-place after all.

"I'd give . . . I'd give *anything* to make it with Ginny." Back in his plate went Ronnie's head, except this time his face was a bit red.

"I don't blame you. She's one good-lookin' babe." I knew he didn't have a chance with Ginny, but I figured I'd best play it straight.

"You don't understand, Sam. That's *all* I ever think about. Daytime, nighttime. Even in my sleep!" Ronnie was practically drooling.

Knowing the hopelessness of the situation, I felt I ought to try and cool him down a bit. But he was too wound up. "You know what I think about?" he said. "I think about how I'd like to . . ." Then Ronnie hesitated. Finally he leaned forward and half whispered. What he said had me in a state of shock. Not that I shock easy, but coming from Ronnie it was some surprise. Boy did he have the hots for that chick. He even told me a few ideas even *I* never thought of!

When Ronnie eventually slowed down, I looked him straight in the eye and said, "Look, man . . . *are* you a virgin?" Ronnie didn't answer at first. Then he gave me a weak nod. The poor frustrated dummy, I thought. Maybe I was going to have to try and do something about that.

I don't know why, but I felt a certain responsibility for Ronnie. Probably because I identified with his social problems, and all the garbage that was going on at school for both of us. That's why I became so much a part of his life . . . and his story. For there *is* a story to tell about Ronnie Finkelhof. You might call it a fairy tale—and yet it really happened. Since I am the only one who experienced it from the beginning, I figure it's up to me put it all down.

CHAPTER

The first time I met Ronnie was on an early morning in September. It was one of those beautiful, brisk fall days, and the leaves were just beginning to turn. Ordinarily a day like that would have put me in high spirits, but it was not a very good period in my life. My family had moved, and I was just starting this new school, feeling alone and lost. That's tough for any kid, but particularly hard for me, considering where I came from. The new neighborhood wasn't my scene, to put it mildly, and I figured I was in for a lonely time.

On that particular morning I was on my way to school, feeling very low, when I saw this boy coming out of a house just a few doors down from where we lived. He was a funny looking kid—tall, gawky, and skinny as a beanpole. He had black straggly hair, and pop eyes that looked even bigger behind thick-rimmed glasses. And he had all these zits on his face. I had seen him before, but we had never spoken. He reached the walk just as I came by, so we could hardly avoid each other.

"Hi," I said.

''Hi,'' he answered. We both knew where we were going, so we kept walking together.

''I'm Sam Bennett. I live up the street with the Wilker-sons.''

''I know,'' he said. ''I've seen you in class. I'm Ronnie Finkelhof.''

That was about the sum total of our exchange. We kept on walking along together, but there was very little conversation. I tried to make some small talk, but Ronnie was not very responsive. What a clod, I thought. Then I began to realize that he was very uncomfortable with me. Somehow I knew it wasn't anything personal. Being black, I'm used to some ofays reacting that way. But in this case I got the feeling that it was different. As I learned later, it was just that Ronnie was extremely shy with everyone. In fact, he was so introverted that it was practically a sickness.

When we got to school that day, kids were milling around outside, enjoying the good weather and waiting until the last minute to head in. But Ronnie went straight to the steps leading up to Randolph Hall. As he turned to give me a ''so long,'' not looking where he was going, he stumbled on the first step and went sprawling, ass over teakettle as my dad used to say—books, notes, and junk flying in every direction. There was an explosion of laughter from everyone, and I heard a kid behind me say, ''It's that drip Finkelhof.'' I felt sorry for the poor guy, and went to help him pick up his stuff. But he didn't seem to want any assistance. He was all red in the face, and grabbed everything in a messy bundle and practically ran up the steps without looking back.

That was my first real contact, if you can call it that, with any student at Mapleton High. But lonely as I was in that sea of whiteys, I wasn't about to take up with the class goon, even if he'd have me. But as things turned out, I kept running into Ronnie on the way to school, just by the accident of timing, and we would walk together, although mostly in silence. Then I noticed that he would be waiting for me in front of his house until I came by. Gradually we started having some dialogue, and before long I began to look forward to seeing Ronnie standing there on his front walk. It wasn't just my loneliness. Ronnie was bright, and the better I got to know him, the more I liked him.

Fact is, Ronnie and I got to be very good friends. We were opposites in almost every respect, but maybe that's what made us interesting to each other. I came from the streets, and my language, style, and whole attitude were different from his. I would tell him dirty jokes—old ones that I thought everyone knew—and he would let go with weird-sounding guffaws. It sounded like laughter was not something that came easy—like it was a whole new thing for him. Anyway, Ronnie gradually loosened up, and before long we were exchanging teenage confidences. Eventually I came to know Ronnie's innermost thoughts and feelings. As a result, I shared every minute of what you might call The Ronnie Finkelhof Legend.

First I should tell you how I came to be living in an upper-middle-class suburban community outside of Chicago, where there weren't too many like me. In fact, I was the only black in the junior class of Mapleton High. The way that happened was that my folks moved to a new job. Pop had always worked in a factory, and up until then we had lived on the South Side of Chicago. Growing up on the streets as I did was not exactly your best environment, and my mom wanted to get me out of there. Our neighborhood had gotten very run-down, and Mom worried about me a lot. So she convinced Pop that they should get work as a couple in a good home, and in an area where I could be in a decent school.

Finding a family that would take a teenage boy along with a couple wasn't easy, so Mom and Pop set their salary well below the going rate. Finally the employment agency got us into this home in Mapleton. It was a beautiful place—especially by my standards—in a quiet residential section on a street lined with fantastic old oak trees. The house was huge, and the servants' quarters had two rooms with a bath in between. It was perfect for us, and the high school was just a short walk away.

Mom was always a great cook, and Pop could fix almost anything, so he made a good handyman around the house. He also did a bit of butlering when the family entertained, and helped Mom in the kitchen and with the housework. My folks didn't have much education, but they were naturally smart, and good people, and the Wilkersons really appreciated them.

But as you can imagine, I was kind of lost. That first week at Mapleton High was a real bummer. None of the kids had shown any signs of being friendly, so I just kept to myself. I figured I was in for a lonely couple of years, until . . . on that bright, sunny fall day on the way to school . . . I met Ronnie Finkelhof.

CHAPTER

3

Ronnie and I found each other because we had no other choice. I had my own social handicap, but I think Ronnie's was even worse. As I said, he was shy—painfully shy. He was anything but good-looking, and too clumsy to get involved in sports. To make it simple, he just had nothing going for him, except that he was a straight-A student. Which didn't help his social life either. So the two of us had something in common, although for different reasons. But apart from that, I really learned to like Ronnie. Too bad the other kids couldn't see anything in him. I guess if they had, though, there wouldn't have been room for me.

As Ronnie and I got to know each other better, I found he talked a lot about his father. Mr. Finkelhof was a man in his early fifties, not very tall, but nice-appearing in a conservative kind of way. Ronnie looked nothing like him, and when they stood side by side, Ronnie towered over him like a gargoyle. I'm sure Mr. Finkelhof must have been sensitive to Ronnie's looks. It was like he came from another union. But the real problem between them went far deeper.

Mr. Finkelhof was a lawyer in a big firm—a partner, with his name in the title. It was Mitchell, Payne, Dillingham, Colter and Finkelhof. I'm not sure that was the

order, but I remember his name was last. He was Mr.
Establishment himself. I never spent much time around
him, but as Ronnie and I got closer, he talked more and
more about their relationship. I remember one day when
we were having a Coke after school, and I asked Ronnie
about college, and what he wanted to do with his life.

"I'm hoping to get into Harvard, and then go on to
Harvard Law School," Ronnie said. "My father's got it
all planned."

"Your father?"

"Yeah, sure. He wouldn't have it any other way."

"You mean he never asked what *you* want to do?"

"Hey, Sam, you don't know my dad. He makes all the
decisions around the house. Anyway, what's wrong with
being a lawyer?"

"Nothing, man. Nothing at all. If that's what you
want." I could see Ronnie was uncomfortable with this
discussion. "You know how *my* pop describes a lawyer?" I asked.

"How?"

"Well, if two guys were fighting over a cow, and one
was pulling on the head and the other on the tail, there
would be a lawyer milkin' it."

Ronnie laughed. I could see that his father was a sensitive issue, and decided I should avoid it. But it was
obviously something very much on Ronnie's mind, and
came up on other occasions, particularly when he needed
his old man's permission to do something we were planning. I gradually got the full picture. Mr. Finkelhof was
the square of all time. That would have been okay, except
that he could not accept any point of view other than his
own. "Dogmatic," I think, is the word. I guess being a
lawyer can make you that way. There is only one answer
to every problem, and the judge decides what it is. In

Ronnie's house, Mr. Finkelhof was the judge. There was no room for give and take, no flexibility. No excuses for not doing what you're supposed to do. No softness, no room for failure. You lived by the book, and that's how it was.

One of Mr. Finkelhof's pet peeves was the younger generation. He had no tolerance for sexual freedom, long hair, rock music, alcohol, or even blue jeans! As for drugs, in his mind anyone caught with them should be sent away for life. Mr. Finkelhof would lecture Ronnie endlessly on the evils of dope. I'm sure he loved Ronnie, and that his attitude came out of concern for his son in those difficult adolescent times. But he just went too far. Not that he wasn't right, but he made no distinction between shooting smack and taking a Valium! I know if I told my pop that I had smoked a joint, he might tell me to be careful, but he wouldn't go through the roof. Not so with old Mr. Finkelhof. There was only one way to do things—his way. His dominance of Ronnie was complete in every respect.

I suppose if Ronnie had been at least a little better looking, with more personality, and had some temptations among his peers, he might have tried to break away. But he had no opportunities in any direction. He wasn't invited to parties, he was not part of any social group, and no girl ever gave him a flirtatious look or the slightest encouragement to come out of his shell. So he just dug in deeper and deeper, and his submission to his father's will became total. I guess you'd say he lived in a kind of fear—of his father, of people, of the world. I'm no psychiatrist, but I could understand the combination of things that made Ronnie the way he was.

Ronnie's mom just went along with her husband, preferring not to interfere. She was busy with her own life, mostly civic activities, charity work, running the house, and like that. I don't think she was much of an influence on Ronnie one way or the other. She was loving, I'm sure, but her husband made all the major family decisions. And then there was Debbie, Ronnie's younger sister, to occupy her attention. Mrs. Finkelhof felt closer to her daughter than her son, and the two females had an easy relationship. Ronnie was left to his dad. I suppose Mrs. Finkelhof thought that's the way it should be.

With all that, Ronnie was nevertheless totally male under his repressions. He had the same wants and desires that any teenager felt, but there was no way he could get them past his thoughts and dreams. That was particularly true when it came to girls. Ronnie wanted a girl in the worst way. I'd been around a little back in my old neighborhood, but I don't think Ronnie even knew what a girl looked like with no clothes on—at least not in any kind of detail! There was that one girl in particular that drove him crazy—Ginny. She was the school beauty, with a figure that you had to turn around and ogle every time she passed. All the kids in school were after her. Ronnie had about as much chance with Ginny as I would have had. Maybe, under the right circumstances, even less! I liked to think that anyway, even if there was no truth to it.

Ginny was an only child. Her father was head of the local bank, and her mother the community's social leader. Theirs was a real WASP establishment family. The father drove a big Lincoln sedan, and the mother a Ford station wagon—naturally. I think they put mayonnaise on everything. You know the type I mean. There was no way you could imagine Ronnie and Ginny having any kind of relationship. It would be like a Woody Allen movie come to life. Ginny was always surrounded by the

Big Men on Campus. The main one was Andy Hamilton, captain of the football team—a six-footer, good-looking, and with an athlete's build. Andy and Ginny kind of went steady, although they never announced it as such. Ginny's parents frowned on any real commitment. But the two did have their moments, although maybe nothing much more than some heavy smooching.

Occasionally Ronnie and I would get out in society— like down to the local ice cream and pizza parlor, a hangout for the high school kids. We always sat alone, had something to eat, and talked just to each other. Mostly the few times Ronnie would agree to go there was to see Ginny. And I mean *see*, because that's all it ever amounted to. And there were always so many guys around her that it was hard to get a clear look. I must say Ronnie had good taste in girls, although from his standpoint I figured Ginny to be in another world. But, in the meantime, I think he got a rise out of her, if you know what I mean.

As I found out, Ginny was not unaware of Ronnie, although it's just as well Ronnie didn't know what kind of awareness it was. Ginny knew she was being watched, and she and Andy made jokes about it. "There's that horse's ass Finkelhof again," Andy would say, followed by a lot of giggles. There was more than one occasion when Andy would get Ginny to walk real sexily past Ronnie while he and his friends watched. They played a cruel game, but Ronnie never caught on. I just kept it to myself.

Ronnie was plain naive about girls and how they react to boys. Young as I was, I figured I was still better experienced at peer relationships than most. And that went for more than boy/girl stuff. Back in my old neighborhood things were nothing like here in Mapleton. In the city I learned to be street smart. I had to if I wanted to survive.

But there was more than that in my background. Growing up for me was an unusual combination of street and home life. My parents didn't have too much schooling, but they had their own kind of wisdom. They were what I guess you'd call God-fearing, church-going folk. Their own parents had instilled in them a sense of decency and honesty that somehow, in spite of the neighborhood influences, had rubbed off on me. My mom in particular was very ambitious where I was concerned. She wanted me to get all the education that she and Pop had missed, and to be able to take advantage of the social changes that were beginning to give blacks a chance in this world.

I understood all that, although I really didn't know what I wanted to do with my life. I just hadn't thought too much about it. I did know that I should begin to consider the future—after all, I was a junior in high school, and the time for decisions was not far off.

Ronnie, of course, had his life cut out for him. He was going to be a lawyer. But I felt sorry for his lack of sophistication in the social way of things, particularly in the female department. He needed an experience. I think he spent a lot of time in the bathroom with the door locked. But that's one thing Ronnie never discussed with me. There was little I could do to help in that area—or in any other way for that matter. I figured he was stuck with his problems, and was doomed to a dull and unexciting existence. How wrong I was!

Then came the day I made the big discovery about Ronnie.

CHAPTER

It was a rainy Friday, and Ronnie had asked me back to his house after school—for the first time. There was no one home, and we went up to his room. It was kind of preppy, with our high school pennant on the wall, a Harvard banner, a DO NOT DISTURB sign on the door, and a NO PARKING sign standing in the corner. It was like Ronnie wanted to be "one of the boys." But the *real* Ronnie was all the books around. The shelves were overflowing, and I had a feeling he had read every one. Ronnie got us some Cokes and we made ourselves comfortable.

"Sam?"

"Yeah?"

"What's it like to be black?"

"You ought to know," I said.

"What do you mean?"

"It's feeling like you're plain out of it, man. You're not accepted—ever—no matter what."

"Hey, Sam, things are different now. . . ."

"Oh yeah? It just *seems* different. It really the hell isn't. All whites are racists, one way or another."

"You think I'm a racist?"

"I think you could be, under different circumstances."

"Sam, you're my best friend. How can you say that?"

"Sorry, Ron. Forget it. I guess blacks have a built-in thing we don't ever forget. But let me ask *you* a question, smart guy. How do you feel about the kids at school?"

"What do you mean?"

"Do they accept you?"

"C'mon, Sam. You know I've got no friends there. Far as I'm concerned they're *all* jerks."

"*All* of them?"

Ronnie didn't answer. He got the point.

"But there's a difference between you and me," I said. "With me I carry my problem *everywhere*—with my bare face hanging out. Like when I was ten some white kid in my class from a better part of town invited me to his birthday party—I think his parents wanted to show they were liberal. Anyway, my mom got me all dressed up, and when I got there with a present under my arm, the doorman said, 'Deliveries in the rear.' I turned around and ran all the way home and cried myself to sleep."

"Wow. What a bummer."

"I can't change the color of my face—but *you* could hack it, Ron."

"How? You know everybody puts me down."

"Get into a school activity—there must be *something* you could do without screwing up."

"Yeah, sure! I went out for track once and knocked down every single hurdle the first time. The story got around the whole school. Then I tried out for the school play. They gave me the part of a soldier in some dumb drama. I ran out on stage with the wrong army, and was left standing in the middle with guys pointing their rifles at me. One wiseacre said later he'd have shot me if he thought I had sense enough to fall!"

"I gotta tell you something, Ron. I think your biggest problem is in class."

"What the hell are you talking about—I'm a straight-A student!"

"Maybe you're a little *too* smart. You even make the teacher look dumb sometimes with your questions."

"Like when?"

"Like when in Science you asked if Newton's Third Law worked the same in a vacuum as it did in the atmosphere. Or like when you asked how come the speed of light is the maximum. Speed is relative, you said, and two light beams passing each other in opposite directions would be going twice that fast in relation to each other."

"What's wrong with that?"

"Plenty! Nobody likes a smartass."

Ronnie was quiet.

I figured I'd better change the subject. "Hey, you play that thing?" I had noticed a guitar sitting in the corner of the room.

"Yeah, kind of."

"Let's hear it," I said.

"Naaaahhhh. I'm not that good."

"You been taking lessons?"

"For a while. It's kind of my hobby. But I never play for anyone."

"You'll play for me, though—right?"

"Forget it!"

"Play, Ron, or I'm goin' home."

"Come on, Sam. I just fool around."

"So fool around—will you quit stalling?"

"Okay . . . one song."

Ronnie picked up the guitar. It was one of those six-string Spanish jobs, and looked like a good one. He kind of held it lovingly for a minute. Then he started to play.

That's when I made the big discovery about Ronnie. He didn't "just fool around" . . . he *played*. Like a pro. Not just chords, but as a solo instrument. He was fantastic. I didn't utter a sound until he had finished.

"You no-good lying fink! You've been holding out on me!"

"What are you talking about?"

"You're good, you dummy. Do you *know* how good you are?"

"You're putting me on . . . you really think so?"

"I *know* so, buddy. What was that you were playing?"

"Something I wrote . . ."

"I want to hear it again. Does it have words?"

"Yeah, I wrote a lyric."

"Can you sing it?"

"Sam, I never sing for *anybody* . . . just myself. And I'm not about to do it now . . . not even for you."

I cajoled, threatened, and generally made an impossible pest of myself. I was determined to get him going. Finally, I said, "I'll sing a song *I* wrote if you'll sing yours."

Ronnie was suspicious. "Let me hear yours first."

I hadn't really written a song, but I had a title. So in my worst voice I sang, "What Could Be Much Nicer Than To Do It Once Or Twicer In The Mooooooooooorrrrrnnnnning . . ."

"Yeah, go ahead. Let's hear the rest." Ronnie was laughing.

"That's as far as I got. Your turn."

"That's a cheat . . . that's no song."

"Ronnie, sing, or I'll lay another one on you—even worse!"

That did it. "Okay, okay, okay." Ronnie finally gave in. "But turn your back—and don't watch."

The song was called "Girl On My Mind." (You know who.) It was a touching lyric, and I was glad my back was turned. I got kind of misty. As for his voice . . . well, it was beautiful. I sat there listening to a lovely, sensitive soul expressing itself with perfect phrasing, and was totally caught up in the mood of it all. When he finished, I turned around. There was Ronnie, with a sheepish grin on his face. It was hard to put the two together.

"Ronnie . . . darn it, Ron . . . you are *fantastic*!"

"Cut the crap, Sam."

"It's no crap. Have you written anything else?"

"Yeah, sure. I write a lot of junk."

"Do some more."

"No way."

"Finkelhof, will you stop with that act. Who you hiding from? It's me . . . Sam . . . remember?"

"My lyrics are personal. I kind of feel exposed . . . even with you."

"Well, get over it. I thought we agreed we wouldn't keep anything from each other. Now I ain't leaving this room until I hear at least three more songs. And I'm gonna watch . . . whaddya think of that, buddy?"

It wasn't easy, but I got him singing. It was funny sitting there watching Ronnie perform. He didn't look like Ronnie. He was so at home with the guitar and his music that it was as if he were someone else. And each song was better than the last. He was right, too—the lyrics *were* very revealing. I felt closer to him than I ever had before.

One thing was for sure. My friend Ronnie had a real natural, inborn musical talent. And yet he wouldn't accept that, and refused to play for anyone. "Only for myself," he said. "And I guess now you, Sam."

Even his parents weren't aware of what Ronnie had going for him. They knew he played, but thought little of it. "Isn't it nice that Ronnie can play the guitar?" his mother would say. But that was about it.

His sister, Debbie, knew better, however, because she would hang around outside his room when he was singing and playing. She was that kind of nosy kid. I guess a few years back you'd have called her a teenybopper. She was sure Ronnie had talent, but he brushed her off when she said he should take his music seriously.

As for me, like they say, I was born with it. I knew good pop music when I heard it, and once Ronnie got used to me listening, I would sit with him in his room for hours. He had a tape recorder, and we would make cassettes of his songs, with him singing and playing the guitar. The songs were mostly pop and folk-rock—sensitive ballads that told a lot about what was on Ronnie's mind. If you listened to the lyrics, you knew what he was thinking. Songs about being lonely, about being a teenager, about the social vacuum in his life, even about me, and what our friendship meant to him. And of course about girls. I once suggested to Ronnie that he let some professional hear his music, but he would have none of it. In fact he got so upset at the idea that I never mentioned it again. But his little sister was not so subtle.

Debbie was kind of cute, although a little on the chubby side. She had chestnut-brown hair, which she wore long, and was into blue jeans and T-shirts with dumb sayings written on them. One thing that bothered me was her voice. It was kind of whiney and high-pitched. And she was a nag. I guess it's that age. But Debbie really liked Ronnie, even though she bugged him a lot. She was the kid sister looking up to an older brother. There was one day Ronnie and I were in his room cutting another tape when Debbie came bursting in.

"Ronnie, I love that song."

"Who asked you in here?"

"You write super songs. I like them all. They're terrif!"

"How would you know?"

"I can hear them from out in the hall. I hear you singing and playing a lot. Your music is as good as anything on the radio. Better. You could make records."

"Go away, kid—that's the dumbest thing I ever heard."

"Really, Ronnie. What do you want to be a lawyer for? Think of it! You might be famous."

"You really are a creep, Debbie. And stay away from my room. I don't want you hanging around here."

Debbie meant well, but she really didn't understand Ronnie.

"Groupie," Ronnie said as he pushed her out the door.

Debbie didn't like that remark at all. She gave him a raspberry, and flounced off down the hall.

And then she did it.

CHAPTER

5

What Debbie did seemed innocent enough at the time. I guess you can't blame her too much, because she had no way of knowing where it would lead. Maybe

she would have done it anyway, but I'm not so sure she
would have if she could have looked far enough ahead.

Anyway, what she did was to go into Ronnie's room
when he wasn't home, and take one of his cassette tapes.
There were so many lying around she knew he wouldn't
miss it. Then she wrote a little note:

President
Jetstream Records
1000 Michigan Avenue
Chicago, Illinois

Dear Sir:

Enclosed is a tape of one of my songs. I wrote the
words and music, and also sing and play the guitar. I
hope you will listen to it because I think it would
make a good record.

Please let me hear from you. I am anxiously waiting for your reply.

Sincerely,

Ronnie Finkelhof
212 Elm Drive
Mapleton, Illinois
(312) 755-4211

You'd figure the cassette would end up in the waste-
basket, or at best sent back unheard with a form letter.
But as fate would have it, it didn't work out that way. It
wasn't until later that I found out what happened.

The president of Jetstream Records was a man who
went by the name of Aben. I don't know if that was his
first or last name, but it's the only one he ever used—at
least that's all anybody ever called him. On the day Ronnie's tape arrived, Aben was having a meeting with his
staff. The discussion was about whether they should sign

a big hot artist who was asking for a whopping advance
and a top royalty. The deal was in seven figures, and
Aben was nervous. He felt maybe the guy had peaked.

"I'd rather spend the money promoting somebody
new," he said.

"Yeah, but who?" said the head of sales. Salesmen
always want things the easy way, like just taking orders
on a big star.

"There's talent everywhere," Aben said. "All you
have to do is find it."

"Yeah, sure—but where? You know the kind of stuff
that comes in here. I can't sell crap, you know." With
that reply, Mr. Sales got up and went out to Aben's secretary.

"What gems came in today, Joan?"

"Only one. I was about to send it back the usual way."

"Let me have it. I've got to straighten out your boss."

Mr. Sales marched back in the office, and said, "Okay,
Aben. Here's a new artist. Let's give it a listen."

"Come on, Barney, I didn't mean the over-the-tran-
som stuff."

But Mr. Sales had to make his point. Of course, what
he had in his hand was Ronnie's tape. Thing was, Debbie, in her haste and fear of being caught, had grabbed
one of Ronnie's recent songs. There were no titles on the
cassettes, and she didn't even know what she was sending. It was a song Ronnie had written as a gag after we
had had one of our more intimate discussions about girls.
The song was good, but not meant for public consump-
tion. We'd had a big laugh about it, because the lyric was
a kind of double entendre, as they say. It went:

>   I'm gonna romance the
>   pants off of you,

> If it's the very last
> thing I do . . .

. . . and so forth. You know the song, so I don't need to
put down the rest of it. Old Mr. Sales stuck the cassette
in Aben's machine, and turned the volume up real loud
like they do at record companies. And out came Ronnie
singing, "I'm Gonna Romance the Pants Off of You."

Aben caught on very fast, and as they used to say in
the business, he "flipped." The song was a natural quick
hit. But more than that, he dug Ronnie's voice . . . and
his guitar playing. "The meeting's over," Aben said.
"I've got work to do!"

It was late afternoon when the call came in, and fortunately it was Ronnie who picked up the phone. Debbie
and he were the only ones home.

"Long distance for Mr. Finkelhof."

"Mr. Finkelhof is not here. Can I take a message?"

"Would you have Ronnie Finkelhof call—"

"*Ronnie* Finkelhof . . . ?"

"Yes, Ronnie Finkelhof. Would you have him call—"

"Miss, I'm Ronnie Finkelhof. But there must be some
mis—"

"Oh. Good. Hold on, Ronnie. This is Jetstream Records in Chicago. Aben would like to talk to you."

"Aben? But—"

"Hello, Ronnie? This is Aben at Jetstream. I got your
tape, and—"

"My tape?"

"Yeah, your tape. The one you sent me of—"

"But I didn't send you any tape."

"Is your name Ronnie Finkelhof?"

"Yes, but—"

"And do you live at 212 Elm Drive in Mapleton?"

"Yes, but—"

"And is your phone number 755-4211?"

"Yes, but—"

"And did you write a song called 'I'm Gonna Romance the Pants Off of You'?"

"Well yes, I did, but how—"

"Okay, Ronnie Finkelhof. I want to have a talk with you."

At that point Ronnie heard a muffled giggle behind him. He turned to see Debbie with her hand over her mouth, doing her best to control her excitement. It didn't take a brick house to fall on Ronnie. He got the picture very fast. He was going to kill that little sister of his . . . as soon as he could get off the phone.

Aben told Ronnie how much he liked his song, and his singing, and his guitar playing. "I want to come out and see you, kid," he said.

"But—but sir . . . I don't think—"

"Look, Ronnie, I know this must be a shock for you. But I'm comin' out tomorrow. You're a lucky boy. About five o'clock—at your house, okay?"

"No—no—not my house. I don't think—"

"Ronnie, are you talking to any other record companies?"

"Oh no. No one. It's just that my folks—"

"Oh, I get it. You want to keep it between us for now, is that it?"

"Well yes, but—"

"Okay, that's fine with me. But I'm comin' tomorrow, so you better give me a place to meet you."

Well, Ronnie finally gave him the address of the local coffeehouse. Said they could sit in a booth and talk there. He wanted to get off the phone in a hurry and get hold of Debbie. But she saw the look on his face and took off.

You have to understand Ronnie's problem. He was scared to death to perform in front of anyone. He couldn't face up to a stranger listening to his songs. And the thought of being interviewed by a big-time record executive was more than he could emotionally handle. That may sound goofy, but you had to know Ronnie. This wasn't your ordinary stage fright, or nervousness. His shyness, his lack of self-confidence were extreme. As I said, it was a kind of sickness.

Then the problem was compounded. Of all the songs he'd written, why did Debbie have to pick *that* one? All about romancin' her pants off! Oh my God, he thought. If anyone hears that . . . That's when I got the frantic phone call. He had to see me right away. He was a basket case.

"You got to help me, Sam. What am I going to do?"

"Ronnie, cool it, man. What's the big deal? You should be flying. Jetstream Records is a hot little company."

"But Sam, I don't want to meet this guy. What will I say?"

"How about letting *him* do the talking?"

"Wait till I get my hands on that Debbie. . . ."

"Ronnie, a guy likes your record, and you go off the deep end—"

"Sam, of all people . . . you know how I am."

"Look, dum-dum," I said, "nobody can make you do anything you don't want to. What's your problem? We'll meet this guy tomorrow, see what he has to say, and then you do as you damn well please. Now cut out the crap."

Ronnie finally calmed down. But I don't think he slept very well that night.

CHAPTER

6

The next day after school I went with Ronnie to meet Aben. When we got to the coffeehouse, it wasn't hard to find him. Sitting in a corner booth was this character with a short beard, who looked to be around thirty-five. He had on blue jeans, and a sport shirt open down about to his navel. He was wearing one of those gold medals on a chain, buried in his hairy chest. This was not local talent! "That's him," I said.

Ronnie held back, but I pulled him over to the booth. "Excuse me, are you Mr. Aben?" I said.

"Yeah, I'm Aben. Sit down, Ronnie. Good to meet you."

"Oh, I'm not Ronnie. My name's Sam. Sam Bennett. I'm just Ronnie's friend. This is Ronnie here."

Ronnie was standing behind me, and I had to move aside so Aben could see him. "Oh," he said. I guess I looked more like what he expected than Ronnie did. Anyway, once we got things straightened out, we both sat down. Aben didn't waste any time, and got right to the point.

"Ronnie, I liked that song you did. Have you written any others?" Aben was obviously interested, but after getting a load of Ronnie, I think he wanted to check things out.

"Well, yeah, I've done more, but—"

"I want to hear them, kid. If they're as good as 'I'm Gonna Romance the Pants Off of You,' maybe we can make a deal."

"Make a deal?" Sometimes Ronnie was slow on the uptake.

"Look, man, I think you have talent, and I might try a few sides with you."

"You mean make a record . . . a record that would be released? Oh, Mr. Aben, I don't think—"

"Aben . . . just plain Aben."

"Uh, Aben . . . I couldn't do that. No one would want to hear *me*. You must be making a mistake."

Aben became more intrigued as he talked to Ronnie.

"Now look, kid, I know a good song and talent when I hear it, and you—"

"But Mr. Aben—"

"Aben, just Aben . . ."

" . . . Aben. Okay, Aben. But you don't understand. I go to school. I'm going to be a lawyer."

"What's that got to do with it, man?"

"I only play for myself. Music is just a hobby."

"Look, Ronnie, this doesn't have to interfere with your studies. It only takes afternoons or evenings to cut an album. You can come into town on Saturdays, or after school, and once it's finished, I do all the rest. You just sit back and wait to see if it's a hit."

"But what if it *isn't* a hit? What if I fail?"

"So? We try again."

"Everybody'd hear me on the radio. What if nobody likes it? I couldn't take that."

"But what if it *does* take off? Why don't you think of *that*? You'd be a big man. You could go on a concert tour and—"

"On a concert tour? Play in front of an audience? Oh, Mr. Aben—"

"Aben . . . just Aben . . ."

" . . . Aben. I could never play in front of people, never. Oh no, it's no good. I don't even let my family hear me. We'd better forget about it. I'm sorry, Mr.—er, Aben, but it's no use. I just couldn't—"

"Ronnie, hold it, hold it. Forget any concert tour. Let's just talk about the record. Suppose—suppose nobody knew who you were?"

"Huh?"

"Suppose you used another name?"

"What do you mean?"

"Ronnie, nobody *sees* what comes out of a record, they only *hear* it. We'll use another name on the label. No one will know it's you."

"Well, I don't know . . ."

"If the record flops, it will be your and my secret."

"But what if it's a hit?"

"We should be so lucky!"

"But what if it *is* a hit?"

"In that case, we'll figure it out from there."

I could see that Ronnie was still upset, so I cut in and told him to relax, that I wanted to talk to Aben alone for a minute. I took Aben over to another booth, and explained about Ronnie, as best I could—what his problems were and what kind of a guy he was. I told Aben I would see that he got some more of Ronnie's tapes, and if he still felt the same way, that he should get a contract ready. I didn't want Ronnie to blow this chance, and I figured that somehow I could handle it.

"I don't know, kid," Aben said to me. "This guy's a bit of a weirdo. Do you think he can hack it?"

"Trust me," I said. But I wasn't very sure myself.

When we got back to the booth, I told Ronnie that everything was going to be okay, and not to worry.

"If I do it, *no one is to know*," he said.

"No one," Aben promised.

Then *I* promised, and we all shook hands. Ronnie didn't look too happy, and I thought Aben didn't look too sincere. I suppose he figured that if Ronnie *did* happen to hit, he'd worry about the secrecy business later. *That* kind of problem he would like!

I got Ronnie to send more tapes, and now Aben was really excited, although he tried to play it cool—I'm sure he didn't want to make too heavy a deal. But Ronnie, being the son of a lawyer, knew something I didn't. A contract signed by someone underage could be broken unless approved by the court. So I reminded Aben, and told him that the agreement better be a fair one. Also, I got a copy of a music trade magazine that had some of the deals made by other companies with big artists. Of course, Ronnie couldn't be compared to them, but outside of advances or guarantees, the contract Aben sent wasn't too bad, particularly in regard to the royalty rate. Aben tried to get publishing rights to Ronnie's songs as well, but we knew enough to hold out on that. I'm not sure how generous Aben would have been under different circumstances. But with Ronnie being a minor and not really wanting to sign a contract in the first place, Aben didn't have much leverage.

Ronnie had asked Aben not to call him directly, but to communicate through me. But as Aben heard more of Ronnie's tapes, he "flipped" again, and was hot on the phone to Ronnie at his house. Fortunately Ronnie answered. Even so, it made him very nervous—he still didn't want his parents to know. The main problem was that song, "I'm Gonna Romance the Pants Off of You," which Aben was planning for the first single.

Then with all the goings-on, Debbie smelled something more happening after that first phone call, and started asking questions. Plus she would know Ronnie's songs if they were ever played on the air. This had to be handled. When it came to Debbie, Ronnie wasn't shy, and he read her the riot act. He told her about the deal, and said that if she opened her big mouth, he would never ever speak to her again—for the rest of his life. As I said, Debbie looked up to her older brother, and she got the message loud and clear. She promised, Ronnie made her swear on her mother's life, and they shook hands. That was that.

CHAPTER

7

Although he felt his secret was safe, for the time being at least, Ronnie worried about not letting his father know what was going on. "I've never done anything like this before, Sam," he said. "I don't feel right about it."

"Why don't you just *tell* your old man," I answered. "What's the big deal?"

"You don't know him. He doesn't listen—and if he did, he'd never understand. I *know* what would happen. He'd order me not to see Aben again, or ever make a

record. Then what do I do? I've already signed a contract—I've made a commitment.''

"Why don't you kind of feel him out? Don't tell him
what you've done. Just try and get an idea of how he'd
react. You never know," I said.

Ronnie didn't think he could handle that. He had a
thing about his dad. Truth is, Mr. Finkelhof was impossible—a stubborn and dogmatic patriarch, and Ronnie
could not communicate with him. Too bad. Ronnie was
insecure enough for other reasons without the problem
of a domineering parent. He was really cowed by his old
man. It bugged me, and I pushed Ronnie to get his back
up. He wasn't a kid anymore, I told him. But Ronnie
would only clam up, and I finally laid off.

But I must have had some effect, because that night
after dinner, instead of going to study as usual, Ronnie
sat down in the living room with his father, who was
about to get into the evening paper.

"Dad?"

"Yes, Ronnie?"

"Could we talk a minute?"

"Sure, son. What's on your mind?"

"Well, you know I've been studying guitar."

"I *should* know. I get the bills every week."

"Well, I wondered how you felt about that? I mean,
do you think it's a good idea for me to get more into my
music?"

"Ronnie, I don't necessarily approve of your taking
lessons in the first place. But if it gives you some relax-
ation from your work, I suppose there's no harm, provided you don't spend too much time at it."

"But I was wondering if I should take it more seriously. I think I'm getting pretty good, and—"

"Ronnie, the most important thing in life is to know

your priorities. You plan to go to Harvard, and then on to law school. That's not an easy road, and you can't afford to divert your energies in any other direction.''

''But Dad, I was just thinking that—''

''I've always lived by two mottoes, son. First, 'You can do anything you want if you want it badly enough.' Second, 'Nothing succeeds like success.' Think about that. If you want to get into Harvard badly enough, you will leave no stone unturned to be number one in your class in high school. And nothing will succeed in getting you into the college of your choice *except* success. There *is* nothing else. If you don't give total attention to your number one priority, you risk not getting it. When you want to devote time to something, ask yourself, 'Will this advance my first choice in life?' If not, then it's a waste, and jeopardizes what you are really after and really want. Understand?''

''I guess so, Dad, but I was just thinking of—''

''One more thing, Ronnie. Practicing that discipline of concentration on your goal will serve you well when you do get to college, and then later on in life. It's in your young years that these habits are formed. You see?''

''I understand, Dad. But why can't I do more than one thing at a time? Why can't I—''

''Look, Ronnie, I know keeping your nose to the grindstone isn't easy. Maybe you think I'm being too demanding, but it's in your own interests. That's a tough world out there, and I want you to be prepared.''

What Ronnie needed was not that kind of advice. He needed someone he could open up to, confide in—to make it simple, a father. I guess Mr. Finkelhof meant well, but he sure as hell didn't get the message. And Ronnie was at a loss as to how to reach him. The old man just droned on. ''Do what you have to do first. Business before pleasure. When you have accomplished what you're after, there'll be time enough for diversions. Believe me, that's the way it will pay off. Anyway, what is all this conversation about? What was it you said you wanted to do?"

By now Ronnie had given up. And he was angry. "Why don't you listen to me!" he wanted to say. "There are things I need to tell you." But Ronnie had had it. The hell with you, he thought, you don't deserve to know. Ronnie was justifying his own fear of a confrontation, and finally could only answer with, "Uh—nothing, Dad. Nothing. I just wanted to talk."

"Good, Ronnie. We should have these talks more often. I like to know what's on your mind. Now shouldn't you be getting to your books?"

Ronnie went to his room, and Mr. Finkelhof back to his evening paper.

CHAPTER

Nothing happened for the next few weeks, and Ronnie settled down. I think he figured he might never hear from Jetstream Records again. But then, of course, the inevitable phone call came.

"Okay, Ronnie, we're all set at this end. I've got a great group together, and the charts are fantastic." It was Aben on the phone. He'd called direct to Ronnie again.

"But—er—Aben . . . don't you think—"

"We'll do 'I'm Gonna Romance the Pants Off of You' first, and for the other nine songs for the album I suggest we use—"

"Uh, Aben, couldn't—"

But Aben just kept talking. He understood Ronnie pretty well by now, and wouldn't give him a chance to stall. "Now don't forget," he said, "we have a deal."

That stopped Ronnie. He had a sense of his word. So it was agreed that the first session would be the following Saturday afternoon, and into the evening if all went well. "Don't worry about a thing, Ronnie. We'll work out the numbers at the session. We'll be on twenty-four-track tape, so there'll be plenty of protection. You don't even have to be around for the postproduction if you don't want to."

Of course, I went along. It was a cloudy, gloomy day, and Ronnie was very silent on the bus ride into the city. He was just plain nervous. Spooked is more like it. The recording studio was in this old building in the Loop, up on the second floor. It was kind of crummy, but it was outfitted like nothing we had ever seen. In the control room it looked like the computer center at NASA, loaded with gadgets and lights of all kinds. A young guy was sitting at the control board fiddling with the dials and switches, and then running out to the studio putting microphones in different positions. In the studio itself were six musicians, some younger, some older. There was a Fender guitar, two other guitars hooked up to all kinds of electronic equipment, drums, a tenor sax, and what looked like a piano, but wasn't. It was one of those electric keyboard instruments. And there was an empty chair in front of a microphone kind of separated from the rest of the group. It was partly blocked off by a three-sided partition screen with glass windows in it. And there was a pair of earphones lying on the chair with a wire leading off to a plug in the wall. It was Ronnie's isolation booth. But to him it might as well have been a gas chamber! He took a look at the whole setup and turned white. Ronnie was about to panic.

Aben was beside him in a flash, and began talking very fast. I hung in there, too. "Now don't worry about a thing, Ronnie," Aben said. "We'll take all the time you need to get things the way you want, and don't forget, we're on tape, and we'll have as many takes as necessary, and we can edit in and out to get the best overall . . ." He just kept rattling on as he walked Ronnie, with his guitar, out to that spot in the studio.

Ronnie was worried that the sound engineer would ask who he was—or the man running the tape machine. And what about all the musicians? Aben just didn't make anything of it. "Here's the kid we're gonna work with," he had said when Ronnie came in. "That's Jerry on the Fender, Kenny and Willie on guitars, Skeets on drums, Monty on tenor, and Lennie on keyboard. Okay, let's run the first one down." And that was it. No name was given for Ronnie. Not that it mattered—everybody just called him "man" anyway. You know musicians. They're out of it . . . except for their music.

Ronnie took his seat, and I stayed in the control room. Funny thing, once Ronnie got into that isolation booth with walls around him, he seemed to relax. He felt more comfortable that way. The group went through the first number, and it sounded awfully good to me. I could see Ronnie just a little bit through the glass frame, and he looked over at us and actually smiled. Then they went for a take, and when Ronnie got his cue, he started to play and sing without any hesitation.

Well, I tell you, that was a thrill. If you've ever sat in the control booth of a recording studio with the sound turned up high, listening to something good on the best equipment in the world . . . well, I guess I "flipped," too. I could have kissed Aben. He had put together the best. It was one thing to listen to Ronnie in his room, and know he was good. But to hear him this way was out of this world.

And that was only take one. Aben and the engineer made some more adjustments to the microphones, and moved a lot of dials. Then Aben went out in the studio, said a few things to Ronnie privately, spoke to the drummer, and came back. "Okay, let's run it down once more." I had thought it was perfect as it was! But Aben did three more takes before he called a break, and on a speaker into the studio, told Ronnie to come into the control room. "Okay, man, let's listen and see what you think."

Ronnie's pop eyes popped even bigger. He had never heard himself except on those little cassette tapes of his. Here his voice was booming out of all those speakers, and the back-up group was fantastic.

"What do you think, kid?" Aben asked.

"It—it's amazing. I never knew one of my songs could sound like that," Ronnie said.

You know, if you take some hit song and play it simply on the piano, it doesn't sound like much, particularly with today's music. Production is everything in records now. But when the song is really good, and the production with it . . . well, that's what was going on here.

"I don't like my phrasing in the second chorus," Ronnie suddenly said. "Could we do it again, Aben?"

"Of course, kid."

"And, uh, Aben, do you mind if I make a change in

what the lead guitar is doing? I have an idea that I think would help.''

''Go ahead, it's your record. Try whatever you want.''

Ronnie went out to the studio and had a conversation with the guitar player. In fact, he showed him what he wanted on his own instrument. Aben and I looked at each other. Was that our Ronnie taking charge? Aben turned up the mike so that we could hear what was going on out there. Ronnie sounded very professional—even sure of himself!

When Ronnie finished with the guitar player, he started on the drummer. We couldn't hear what he was saying then, but it was clear the drummer understood what he wanted, and there was no argument. Ronnie the band leader! But then, why not? Music was the one place where he was comfortable with himself.

When Ronnie finished, he nodded to Aben and they did another take . . . and another and another, until finally Ronnie was satisfied. Then the next number. We were in that studio for six solid hours, and finished only two songs. Ronnie apologized for taking so long.

''You kidding?'' Aben said. ''Some of my production groups spend a month on one song. They don't have the real basic talent to know what they're doing until they finally find a sound by fiddling around in the studio forever, running up tremendous bills in the meantime.'' Aben was delighted with the session, and even the musicians, in their cool way, were impressed.

After the group left, Ronnie asked the engineer if he would show him what all the dials were for, and how the system worked. The engineer was a young guy, probably about twenty-four or -five. Aben told us he used him on most of his sessions.

''Sure, man,'' he said. ''It's not as complicated as it

looks. We're recording on magnetic tape, right? It's got twenty-four tracks, or channels, you could say.''

"Why twenty-four? Stereo is only two-track."

"Gives you flexibility. Let's say after the session is finished and the musicians have gone home, and the producer says you've spent enough money already, you decide the vocal sucks. You just rerecord the vocal on that one separate track, and the rest stays the same."

"Hey, that's great. What if you don't like something in the band?"

"Same thing, kind of. You can control the level of each instrument or section, and change the balance any way you want. They're all on their own separate tracks."

"I don't mean to be a pest, but—"

"No sweat, man."

"What are all those other dials on the control board?"

"That's your EQ controls."

"EQ?"

"Equalization. The highs and lows you put on the tape. Frequency response. Then we got the echo control for each track—the amount of room tone we put in electronically. Hey, man, didn't you ever make a record before?"

"Well, no. Do you mind if I ask you one more question?"

"Shoot."

"You got seventy-two dials to control on that board. How do you do that with only two hands and ten fingers?" Ronnie asked.

"It's no big deal. We record everything flat, and after the session is finished, we set each track at the level, EQ, and the amount of echo we want, one at a time, and then dub it all down to two tracks. That's the stereo master."

"One more?" Ronnie was hesitant about taking the

engineer's time, but he didn't seem to mind. "What happens after that?"

Aben cut in. "That's where I take over," he said. "We cut the lacquer master at our own facilities at the office. It's nothing more than an LP record, except that you never play it. We send it back to a pressing plant in the East, and they make the metal parts. Then into the press, and out comes a vinyl record every twenty seconds. If it's a hit, they get shipped out fast. If it's a bomb, we eat them."

"You think you'll have to eat mine, Aben?"

"I don't think so, kid. I don't think so."

Ronnie and I rode back on the bus together. He was more animated than I had ever seen him.

"Sam, that was kind of a gas, the whole thing."

"You dug it, right?"

"Well, yeah. It's a kick to hear yourself with all that stuff going on behind you. I think I'll do "Please Be Close to Me" next. What do you think?"

"Yeah, that sounds okay."

"I want some strings on the next session. You think Aben would go along?"

"Why don't you ask him?"

"I will. Hey, I may get to like making records!" Ronnie was really getting into it all. "It's—it's outrageous, man!"

The next session was the following Saturday. This time it went even faster and better. Aben was flying high, and Ronnie acted like he'd been doing this all his life. He seemed to be in his own private world, singing, playing, and creating. Ronnie was excited—more important, in control—maybe for the very first time. This was *his* session, and he enjoyed that. No one to tell him what to do, to put him down, to laugh at him. He was being taken seriously . . . respected. It gave him a brand-new feeling . . . confidence!

The album was finished in three more weekends—all but the final editing. Ronnie insisted on being present for that, and Aben didn't argue. He had great respect for Ronnie's ear by now, and they worked very smoothly together. Ronnie had never experienced this kind of relationship, and it gave him a tremendous boost.

Ronnie stayed for the final dub-down to the two-track, and then went into town when they cut the lacquer master. He was really caught up in it, and wanted to be sure the equalization and balance were just right. I went along with him for the whole thing, but I felt kind of useless. And after a while, listening to those same songs over and over and over as they worked on them got to be something of a bore. I suppose it was different for Aben and Ronnie—they were involved.

The thing finally got done, and was sent to the plant. Now the art work for the album had to be made. And Aben needed a name to put on the cover. I guess Ronnie had not thought about that.

What were they going to call him?

CHAPTER

7

     Aben made a pass at Ronnie about using his own name. Things had gone so well at the recording sessions that he figured the whole coffeehouse talk no longer had any meaning. Aben probably didn't take it too seriously in the first place. But he miscalculated. Ronnie hadn't changed one bit, and the conversation threw him for a loop all over again. Aben backed off, apologized, and promised he would keep his agreement. But the damage had been done. Ronnie was back in the real world, not isolated in a recording studio. And there was still that embarrassing song—at least to him.

"Sam, I shouldn't have made those records. I shouldn't have signed that contract." Ronnie was having one of his anxiety attacks.

"Ron, stop the garbage. Why don't you—"

"I can't. I can't, Sam. That bastard Aben did this to me. He's going to put those records all over the place and nobody will like them, and I'm going to look like an idiot."

"You really are a case, buddy. Those records are first-rate. So what if they don't sell? That's Aben's problem. Nobody can say your stuff is bad no matter what."

"I'd like to curl up in a ball and disappear."

"Good idea. You curl up in a ball and disappear. Me, I gotta go do my homework."

That got a laugh from Ronnie—or more like a nervous giggle. But it helped. It was up to me to get him out of this state, like always, so I told him another dirty joke. He finally calmed down. There were occasions when I wondered if he was worth it. He really was a chore at times. But then he *was* my friend, and the annoyances passed quickly. Good friends are hard to come by.

Fortunately, we didn't hear anything for almost three weeks, which gave Ronnie a needed pause. But then Aben called and said he had to see Ronnie right away. So we went into town after school.

Aben's office was as big as a large living room, and there was stuff everywhere: records, tapes, lacquer dubs, books, trade papers piled up. His desk was as wide as a dining room table. There were two different phones on it. One was red, and the other had four different lines, with the lights blinking on and off all the time we were there. He had two secretaries in the outer office, probably saying he wasn't in!

Aben was in a good mood, almost like he was on a high. When we came in, he gave Ronnie a big hug, put his arm around me, and said, "Guys, wait till you see what I've got to show you. C'mon, we're going over to the art department."

As we walked out of the office, Aben's secretary said, "Aben, the Pittsburgh distributor has been trying to reach you—they say it's important."

"Not now, honey. Give it to Barney." We almost had to run to keep up with Aben as he led us down the hall, past a lot of offices, most with loud music coming out of them.

The art department was a large room with fluorescent lights, and a couple of long tables with sketches all over.

There were only two people there, a Japanese guy with long hair, and a cute girl with short hair. They were sitting at drawing boards working. Aben didn't introduce us. He just picked up a big folder, and hustled us back to his office.

"You ready, guys?" he said. Then he undid the folder, opened it up on his conference table, stood back, and said, "Get a load of that!"

It was the cover for Ronnie's album. On it was a drawing of the Roman Colosseum, looking down from above. The place was filled with people, and in the center of the arena, believe it or not, was a rock group, complete with modern electric instruments: amplifiers, speakers, the whole works. A rock group in the middle of the Colosseum! But it was the title that was the real shocker. Printed in large, old-fashioned letters at the top was SPARTACUS. That's all it said.

Ronnie and I looked at each other. We didn't know what to say. Finally Ronnie said, "Spartacus? Who's that?"

"That's you, kid," Aben said with a grin. "That's what we're calling you."

Ronnie for sure wasn't pleased. But then he couldn't very well object. He had told Aben he could call him whatever he wanted, as long as it didn't sound anything like "Ronnie Finkelhof." And "Spartacus" could not be argued about on that score. Ronnie didn't want to hurt Aben's feelings, so he just kind of looked at me, and then finally said, "Yeah, sure Aben. That's great." So "Spartacus" it was.

Neither Ronnie nor I knew at the time why Aben had picked that name. It seemed pretty silly to us, because it certainly had nothing to do with the music. But none of the big recording groups over the years ever had names that made any sense. Jefferson Starship, Led Zeppelin, Kiss, Wham!, REO Speedwagon. I guess Spartacus was no worse, so we let it go at that. Actually, Aben was looking ahead. Far ahead. If Ronnie knew at the time what Aben had in mind, I think that would have been the end of the whole deal, right then and there.

After that everything was put to bed. Aben sent the art work off to the printer. They had to make four-color plates, which takes time. And then Aben had to prepare the "liner," which is the back of the album. Usually they put a picture of the artist there, particularly if it's not on the cover. He couldn't do that, so it was just a lot of meaningless words about this great new artist, and how Spartacus wrote all the songs himself, and stuff like that. It said nothing about where he came from or really anything about him, but at least all the song titles were listed.

Aben had said the album wouldn't be out for a few months. School was over, and he didn't want to release it in the summer. Said it was a bad time, and that he wanted to put it out in September and get it into the dealer's stores for the fall market. So we went home to wait.

Ronnie was now freaking out again. The reality of the record release was getting closer. So good buddy Sam had to hold his hand some more. We went to a record store and looked at the competition. When Ronnie listened to some of the current hits, he felt a little better. Most of them were pretty crappy. Ronnie's favorite was an oldie called "American Pie," by Don McLean. Ronnie played the thing a hundred times. I still remember the lyrics:

Bye, Bye Miss American Pie
Drove my Chevy to the levee but the levee was dry

Them good ole boys were drinkin' whiskey and rye
Singin' this'll be the day that I die . . .*

The words seemed to hit Ronnie somewhere.

For the month of August the Finkelhofs always went
to a place they had up on a lake. It was fortunate timing
for Ronnie. Getting out of the city and away from Aben
at that point was good for him. Getting away from me
made sense, too, because all we talked about was the
coming of Spartacus. Ronnie needed to forget things for
a while—I might even say the same for myself!

August for me was working the checkout counter at
the supermarket. It was hot and humid, and it entered
my mind that I could have used some lake time, too. But
nobody had asked me. I wonder if it would have been
the same if I were white. (Don't feel sorry for yourself,
Sam.)

Ronnie got back at the end of the month. He was all
tanned, and the sun had helped his zits a lot, so he didn't
look too bad. We still hadn't heard from Aben, and just
hung out together, wondering if he had changed his mind
about putting out the album. But he finally called Ronnie
and said very matter-of-factly that the release date was
set for September 6, right after Labor Day. That was
without so much as a "How you doin'?" or "You okay?"
He went on to say that the single record of "I'm Gonna
Romance the Pants Off of You" was coming out first,
and then the album just two weeks later, and that he
would send over a couple of copies. Ronnie felt Aben
was very businesslike, and it upset him. Aben had let
down with his "Artist Relations." Maybe he forgot what
he was dealing with; or maybe it was just a pressured,
busy day.

---

*© 1971 Mayday Music/Benny Bird Songs. Used by permission.

Anyway, that shook us awake. The summer had made the whole thing seem remote and unreal. But things got real very fast, because the single and album did indeed come out right on time. I'll say this for Aben, he didn't do things in a small way. The promotion campaign was a big one. There were ads in the music magazines, and, we were told, a lot of window displays in the major cities. There was even a television spot showing the Colosseum in Rome while you heard part of the record, and commercial radio spots that we caught on a Chicago station. Ronnie, of course, couldn't show his face, or I'm sure Aben would have had a video on MTV as well. Disc jockey airplay wasn't much, although we did hear the single a couple times on WLS.

But as far as we could tell, there was very little happening. Ronnie and I went down to the local record store, and they didn't even have a copy in the place. "Oh yeah," the clerk said. "I did have one call for that. I'll order it special if you want." We left.

Ronnie wasn't sure if he was disappointed or relieved. Aben had said it takes time to break a record—sometimes as long as six months. It had only been three weeks.

And then it happened!

CHAPTER

10

⭐

"I'm Gonna Romance the Pants Off of You" took off, as Aben put it, "like a bird." We didn't even know until he called and told us the news. "Every radio station in the country is picking up on it." Aben said. "Reorders from the stores are coming in from all over. It's 'Bubbling Under' in *Billboard*. It's a 'Pick' in R and R." We didn't know what all that meant, except I never heard him so excited. "It'll be on the charts next week for sure. It's gonna be a smash, a super mother of a smash!"

I guess when you've been in the record business for a long time like Aben, you can get the signs early. In any event, he was right. Suddenly you couldn't turn on any Top 40 radio station without hearing Ronnie. Three weeks later, "I'm Gonna Romance the Pants Off of You" was the Number One single record on all three trade-paper charts, and within two weeks after that the Spartacus album was Number One on the album charts. Aben said it was good for at least five million copies domestic, and an equal number international. Jetstream Records had all these deals where foreign companies released their records, and the minute it hit the charts in the United States, they all jumped on it. Spartacus made the Top 10 in West Germany, England, France, Italy, Japan, and

Australia. Aben said he hadn't seen anything like it since the Beatles.

At first Ronnie acted very cool about it all. But the truth is, he was in a daze. He didn't seem to want to talk about it much, and I didn't push him. It was our senior year in high school, and we went about our business as if nothing was any different.

But of course it *was* different. First there was Debbie. She became a total pain. She went bananas. She was so excited she couldn't contain herself.

"Ronnie, isn't it super?"

"Debbie—"

"It's absolutely the most fab thing that's ever happened in this whole town. I can't wait until—"

"Debbie, will you cool it?"

"When are you going to tell, Ronnie?"

"Not now."

"When? When, Ronnie?"

"I don't know. Maybe never."

"Darn you, Ronnie. You're teasing."

"I'm not, Debbie. I just don't want it out yet."

"But you're a big hit. The whole school is talking about Spartacus. Please, Ronnie. Let me tell Sally. She's my best friend. She won't say a word to anyone. I'll make her promise."

"Debbie, if you tell so much as one soul . . . if you even say the word Spartacus in your sleep . . . I'll—I'll—I'll do something so terrible it will be the sorriest day of your life."

"What about Mom? She keeps asking me what I'm grinning about all the time."

"No!"

"Dad . . . ?"

"*Double* no! Now forget it and bug off!"

"Ronnie, you're—you're—you're a no-good miserable nasty creep, and I hate you." That outburst was followed with her last-resort insult—sticking out her tongue at him. Then she knew enough to get out of there fast.

"Don't you forget," Ronnie yelled after her. "You promised. You *promised*," he screamed. Something was going to have to be done about that little pest.

Aben had a much more serious problem than little sisters. Ronnie hadn't changed his mind about the secrecy business, and Aben didn't dare go back on his word or bring the matter up. At least not right now. But what to do? You can't have a new overnight superstar hidden in a closet. Every disc jockey in the country wanted Spartacus on his show. The media was asking for pictures and a bio. "Where's the press kit? What kind of a joint are you running?" Aben was getting calls by the hundreds.

Then, of course, there were the agents. The William Morris office called Aben twice a day, Creative Artists Agency even more. Concert promoters kept upping their offers—they thought Aben was playing hard to get. TV guest shot proposals came in by the dozens, and there was even a feeler from Hollywood. Something had to be done.

I have to say Aben was bright. His success in the business was no accident. And he solved this problem, too—at least for the moment. In fact, he turned it into a kind of asset. The story was released that Spartacus would not identify himself. He would make no appearances—anywhere. "I want to make records," he was quoted as saying. "I am not interested in the public life." Aben made him sound like a male Greta Garbo!

Spartacus became known as the "mystery man." The jockeys picked up on it; so did the trade papers, the press, fan magazines. Speculation ran rampant. It was like the whole PR and promotion campaign had been planned that way from the beginning. Aben now had a story with which to respond to all the media, and the pressure on Ronnie relaxed somewhat. His secret was being protected and handled. But as we learned later, the press doesn't give up easily.

Ronnie was kept busy with school and writing new songs. Aben wanted to get the next album ready, although he didn't want it released for a while. In the meantime, he kept putting out new singles from the first album, spaced very carefully, and it seemed like each one was bigger than the last. Funny thing, the rest of the songs were not at all like "I'm Gonna Romance the Pants Off of You." They were much better, really. Now that Aben had broken Spartacus with the gimmick song, each one after that automatically got big airplay and attention. That album had songs in it that have become classics: "Sixteen," "The Girl I Care for Doesn't Care for Me," "Lonesome Day, Lonesome Night," "Come Into My Life"—you know them. The kids really dug every one, and even the adult world acknowledged Spartacus as a talent and a poet. He had great reviews in *Time*, *Newsweek*, and all the music magazines.

Those were strange times for Ronnie. He didn't know who he was or who he wasn't. Some days, in his head, he lived the dream of being Spartacus. Then something would happen that reminded him that nothing had really changed in his life. I remember a day in physics class when Ronnie opened up with one of his weird ideas. Mr. McKibbon was talking about the structure of matter, and how the atom is the smallest unit.

"But sir"—Ronnie always started out that way—"isn't it possible that the neutron is like a sun, and the electrons around it like planets, and there could be a whole universe within matter itself—just like our sun might be a neutron, and the planets electrons circling it as part of matter in another world . . . ?"

The class laughed. I liked Ronnie's wild imagination—probably part of what made him a writer—but the kids at school put him down at times like that. And that would pop Ronnie's Spartacus bubble and bring him back to reality—whatever reality was for him. The poor guy didn't know which way to turn. So he just retreated into his shell.

There was no place else to go.

CHAPTER

11

"Sam, I wish I could meet a girl who would like me." Ronnie and I were having a burger after school when he hit me with that.

"What's to stop you, buddy?"

"Very funny! Sam, I've got to tell you. I daydream about Ginny like every minute. Then I dream about her at night."

"Forget about that one, Ron."

"I know . . . What's it like, Sam?"

"What's what like?"

"You know, having a girl."

I had to laugh. "That's a tough one to answer."

"How many have you had?"

"Oh, a couple hundred."

"Come on, really. How many?"

"Maybe six or seven, but more than once each."

"Oohh, man. Oooooooooooohhhh, man!"

Ronnie had been talking more than ever about girls, and I really felt sorry for him. He needed an experience badly. I figured there was nothing I could do to help. But then on second thought, maybe there was. I knew this chick in Chicago named Darlene, although I hadn't seen her for a while. I remembered she had a friend in the same apartment building and that they used to hang out together. Both of them worked at Mercy Hospital. Darlene's friend was kind of kookie, but she was fun, and they were good buddies.

"How about we double date?" I said.

"What are you talking about?"

"I've got a friend in Chi who has a friend."

"You crazy?"

"I'm serious."

"No way."

"My friend's name is Darlene. She's got skin the color of chocolate milk and a figure out of this world."

"Bully for you!"

"And her friend has a figure to match."

"Forget it, man."

"Her friend is white."

"Knock it off, Sam! That's not what I was worried about."

Ronnie was getting red in the face. "Look," I said, "you can't just go out and make it with some chick right off the bat. You've got to start someplace. You need experience just *talking* to a girl." Ronnie didn't answer.

"You might even score with Marsha—that's Darlene's friend—once she gets to know you."

"That's the problem—getting to know me!" Ronnie's image of himself never ceased to amaze me.

"Ronnie, will you loosen up," I said. "Marsha's easy. She's real cool—no way uptight. And if she digs you—"

"She won't." Ronnie was nervous just talking about a date.

"But you'll go?"

"I didn't say that."

I knew what Ronnie really wanted, but he just kept shaking his head. I could see it was up to me. So that night I gave Darlene a call. I figured I'd just tell her the truth about Ronnie's problem and what I was up to. Marsha was there, and they both got on the phone.

"Sam, I haven't heard from you since you moved. And now you come up with this stupid idea." Darlene was just putting me on. I knew she'd like to see me.

"Sounds like it might be kicks," Marsha said.

"Sure. Ron and Marsha. We'll have some fun. Whaddya say, girls?"

A little more horsing around, and a date was set. Now I had to deal with Ronnie. It wasn't easy getting him on the bus into the city. And then it wasn't too hard either. He really wanted me to make him go, but he was as nervous as a jumping bean on a hot skillet. Right up to the time we got to the apartment Ronnie was ready to turn back. But we finally made it.

We went straight to Marsha's place. Ronnie was in a sweat as we rang the bell. Darlene was there and opened the door. As I said, I hadn't seen her for a while, and if anything, my memory didn't do her justice. She was about five foot seven, had a beautiful complexion.

She had on a sheer white dress, and I mean she was something to look at.

"Hi, stranger," she said. "Come on in."

"This is my friend Ronnie. . . . Ronnie, Darlene."

"Hi, Ronnie."

Ronnie managed a "Hi" in return.

Marsha came out of the bedroom as we came in. She still had that kookie look, but she also looked pretty good. I hoped Ronnie would think so.

Marsha had very straight, long blond hair, and was about Darlene's height. Her figure wasn't quite as good, at least by my standards. I don't think she was wearing a bra under her beige cotton blouse. I looked over at Ronnie to see his reaction, but his eyes were on the floor.

After the introductions, we sat down. Darlene and Marsha each had some white wine, and I had a beer. Ronnie had a Coke. I would like to have given him a belt of Old Burning Stump, or some kind of cheap strong booze to relax him, but he didn't drink. There was small talk, but mostly between the girls and me. Marsha kept eyeing Ronnie, and smiling at him with a sexy look. I knew she got the picture, and I had a feeling she might go all the way if we left them alone. Maybe she liked the idea of breaking in a virgin. Or maybe she just dug distortion. It's hard to tell. With some girls sex is like saying "how do you do." But then I shouldn't be unfair. Maybe she just felt sorry for the poor guy. At any rate, I knew it was time for Darlene and me to take off. By the way she looked at me, I knew Darlene was thinking the same thing.

"Hey Sam, you haven't seen the way I've redone my apartment."

"When did you do that?"

"Just finished it last month. Come on. I want to show you."

As we got up, Ronnie got up, too. The dummy was going to come along, but Marsha caught on very fast. She got up and put an arm through Ronnie's.

"Don't go, Ronnie. Stay here with me." The look she gave him would have turned on a eunuch!

That was our cue, and Darlene and I were out the door before Ronnie could say a word—he was speechless anyway. We went down to her apartment. I figured maybe I could get in a little action myself, but she held me off. "Hey, Sam, it's been a long time. I don't go at it like that!" I should have known better with her. But she didn't get angry—we just sat around, talking about Ronnie, about old times, and had a nice visit. After an hour or so, I figured we'd better rescue my friend upstairs.

Before we even got to Marsha's apartment we could hear the music. Ronnie and Marsha were playing records, and as we came in, they were talking up a storm. Darlene and I looked at each other in surprise—the two of them hardly even noticed us. Ronnie was telling Marsha all about the group they were listening to. He knew every sideman on the recording, what other records they had made, and their whole history. Marsha was a music lover, and she was fascinated. They had found something in common, thank God!

The four of us sat around talking for a while, although once we got off music, Ronnie clammed up. Marsha kept looking at him in a funny way—I think she was trying to figure him out. But when it was time to leave, she gave him a kiss. "Bye, hon," she said. "I hope we'll see some more of each other."

Ronnie was stunned for a minute. "That would be nice," he finally stammered. Then we took off.

Ronnie didn't have much to say on the bus ride home, and I decided it was best not to push it—about his reaction to Marsha and the whole afternoon, I mean. But when I dropped him off at his house, he said, "Hey Sam, I think Aben can get us tickets to the rock concert next week. Do you think the girls would like to go?"

I knew the day had been a success—or at least a beginning!

CHAPTER

12

It was about that time that Aben called with a problem. It's the kind of problem I would like to have. The ten million albums worldwide Aben had figured Spartacus would sell looked more like fifteen million. Ronnie's royalty came to about a buck an album. Not even counting the single records, that was fifteen million dollars right there. Then there were the songs that Ronnie wrote, words *and* music. He owned the copyrights, and the license fees came to forty cents an album. Again not counting the singles, that was another six million dollars.

There was more on top of that. Aben said Ronnie should join ASCAP, and collect the performance fees paid by all the radio stations and other places that performed his music. As Aben explained it, there are two performance societies, ASCAP and BMI. They monitor the use of music throughout the country, and have arrangements for the same to be done all over the world. Every time one of Ronnie's songs was played on the radio, on television, in a concert, on a jukebox—anywhere—Ronnie would get paid. It would amount to hundreds of thousands of dollars a year as he kept writing, and probably indefinitely after that as his songs became standards. Ronnie told me one day he was in the dentist's office when he heard one of his songs coming over the wired music system. "I'm even making money while this guy is drilling my tooth," he said, and laughed.

There's still more. Contracts could be entered into for sheet music, and all the big print companies were bidding for the rights—piano copies, orchestrations, folios—even band arrangements.

"The money will be coming in soon," Aben said. "And it's got to be handled."

But where was it to go? It couldn't very well be put in Ronnie's bank. That would be funny, Ronnie walking up to the teller at the neighborhood branch where he had a savings account with two hundred and forty dollars in it, and saying, "Excuse me, miss, I'd like to make a deposit." "Sure, Ronnie, how much this time?" she might ask. "Uh, twenty-one million for today, but I'll be in next week with more."

Aben told Ronnie he had to retain a lawyer—there was no other way. Ronnie agreed. But where to go? He still wasn't prepared to tell his father, and he felt it would be disloyal to go to someone else. Also, he wanted a lawyer he could trust to look after his interests. So he went to Dan Colter, one of his father's partners in the firm. It made him feel that would make it okay when he had to face up to his family.

Mr. Colter was, I guess, about sixty. Ronnie said he

had never seen him in anything but a gray or blue suit with a white shirt and dark tie, even when he came over to his father's house on a Sunday afternoon. Colter handled mostly corporate matters in the firm, and he was straight as an arrow. He turned down a lot of cases because he didn't consider them totally honorable by his standards. You know the type. Square by our way of thinking, but highly respected in the community.

Colter had known Ronnie since he was a baby, and never failed to remember a birthday, or to send him a Christmas present. He was like an uncle, but Ronnie would never think of ever calling him anything but "Mr. Colter."

"Hello, Ronnie. My secretary said you had something important to discuss with me—in confidence," Mr. Colter said. Ronnie was sitting across from him at the desk in his big paneled office.

"My father always told me about the total privacy between a lawyer and his client."

"Absolutely, Ronnie. You'll learn that in your first year of law school. The lawyer/client relationship is inviolable. A lawyer may not be required to divulge client information even in a court of law. It's privileged. Why do you ask?"

"I want to retain you as my counsel."

"Ronnie, are you in trouble?"

"Not really. But I need help. And I can pay you."

"I'm not worried about that, Ronnie. But you put me in a spot. Until I hear what you have to say, I don't know if I'm prepared to accept a confidence that I would be required to keep from your father. After all—"

"I need you, Mr. Colter. If you can't—"

"Ronnie, why don't you tell me what this is all about, off the record, as a friend."

"I'm sorry, Mr. Colter, I can't do that. I either speak to you as client to lawyer, or there's not much more to say."

"Ronnie, I don't think I can accept that. Why can't we—"

At that point Ronnie got up from his chair and started for the door. "Thank you, Mr. Colter. I understand your problem. Please say nothing about this to my father."

"Ronnie, please . . . don't leave yet."

"Mr. Colter, I need a lawyer. And I'm sure I won't have a problem finding one to take me on. Seriously, I do understand how you feel. It's just that I didn't want to go—"

"Ronnie, come back here. And sit down. I can't allow you to go to outsiders. I would never forgive myself if anything went wrong and I had to face your father later. All right. I'm your lawyer. I only hope I'm doing the right thing. Now what's this all about?"

Ronnie told Mr. Colter the whole story, from beginning to end. I guess lawyers are used to hearing unusual cases, but this was the topper. And so close to home. Ronnie told me Colter just sat there with his mouth hanging open. "You're *Spartacus*? *You* are Spartacus? I don't believe it! I just don't believe it!"

It took Ronnie a while to convince old man Colter that he wasn't pulling his leg. The attorney knew all about Spartacus, even if he didn't buy records. *Everyone* did. As I said, it was like Elvis—or the Beatles. Well, Colter finally settled down. Ronnie reminded him of the confidentiality of their relationship. The man wasn't happy. He wasn't happy at all. Ronnie had boxed him into a corner. He tried to convince Ronnie to bring his father into their confidence, but Ronnie just wasn't ready. "Later . . . sometime . . . but not now," he said. I guess

Colter figured he'd have to bide his time. Eventually he would get the boy to come around.

"There will be sizable money coming in," Colter said. "How do you propose we handle it?"

"I've thought about that." Ronnie looked concerned. "I wouldn't know *how* to deal with it. It scares me. Is there any way I could have nothing to do with the money—I mean for the time being at least?"

"We could set up a trust, an irrevocable trust. If you are willing to make me trustee, it will be out of your hands completely. In fact you could not touch a penny without my approval."

Ronnie thought for a minute. Finally he said, "That's what I want, Mr. Colter. I get an allowance from my father. I don't need any more money. I don't want to change things at home, or be tempted to do anything I shouldn't be doing. It could be dangerous. I want to keep up with my studies and go to college and law school. Okay! Do it! Tie up the money so I can't touch it. And no matter what I ever ask you for . . . I don't care what it is . . . turn me down. Please. I mean it."

"I'm glad that's how you feel, Ronnie," Colter said. "Frankly, I wouldn't have it any other way. The responsibility you have handed me is bad enough without the added risk of what all that money might do to you. Now what about my fees? This will take time, and I have a responsibility to my partners."

"Whatever you say," Ronnie said. "Do whatever you would do with anyone else."

Colter went right to work. He set up a Spartacus trust, and Ronnie signed it, making Colter trustee. The attorney had total and exclusive power to act for all the Spartacus affairs, and could be a cover for the real owner of the assets. A Spartacus bank account was opened, and as the money rolled in, it was invested. Stocks, bonds, real estate deals, everything. Mr. Colter knew his business. He set up a music publishing company to handle all of Ronnie's songs, and made print deals for sheet music, subpublishing rights with foreign companies, and ASCAP membership for the firm. Somehow he even managed to get Ronnie writer-membership in ASCAP under the name Spartacus, care of the Spartacus trust at the address of the law firm. He was able to file federal and state tax returns under the trust name. Between all the income pouring in, and Colter's smart investments, Ronnie became a multimultimillionaire. If you've ever wondered how much money rock stars make, just add up all that loot. And so far all from only one album!

"Please, Ronnie, let me tell your dad," Mr. Colter pleaded.

"Not yet. I have to do it myself. But I'm not ready. Be sure and pay the firm your fees from the trust. Don't forget, you're my lawyer." Colter was trapped. And Ronnie was adamant.

All this time Ronnie was living the same way as always. There were no expenses against that tremendous income except for legal fees. No agent, no personal manager, no high living. Just money on money piling up. Colter had to hustle to find places to invest it fast enough.

At home Ronnie got ten dollars a week from his father. Truth is, that allowance had always seemed on the short side, what with the way prices were going up. Under the circumstances, it became increasingly frustrating for Ronnie to have to deny himself the few small things he wanted and couldn't afford. So in spite of his resolve not to let his hidden wealth be an influence in any way, he mustered up a little new-found courage and decided to hit the old man for a raise.

"Dad, another five a week would sure be a help."

"What would you do with it?"

"Not much more than I'm doing now. You know what inflation is. Movies cost five dollars. A Coke is sixty cents at most places. I just barely get by."

"Ronnie, maybe you have to cut down on movies . . . and Cokes. Do you have any idea what it takes to earn the kind of money I do?"

"Maybe I should try and earn some myself." Ronnie thought that was a good joke.

"You? First of all, I don't want you doing anything that would interfere with your studies. You'd have to work too many hours, and that would be at minimum wage."

"I think I could manage to do better than that," Ronnie said. He was beginning to enjoy this conversation.

"Ronnie, don't be ridiculous. Why do you think I'm planning law school for you? Without an education you couldn't keep yourself in chewing gum! As for your allowance, it's good experience for you to learn how to budget. Wait until you have to earn your own money, and see how hard it is. Money doesn't come easy, you know."

"Okay, Dad. I guess you're right." It was a temptation to tell him right then and there, but he quickly put that thought out of his head.

Ronnie and I had a good laugh about it later. "I can always get some money from Colter," Ronnie said. "He won't hold me to our deal for just a few dollars."

But he turned out to be wrong.

CHAPTER

13

It became public knowledge that the firm of Mitchell, Payne, Dillingham, Colter and Finkelhof represented Spartacus, and Mr. Colter was besieged with inquiries and offers. His partners, including Mr. Finkelhof, were curious about how he came to have a rock star client. The firm was hardly known for that kind of representation, and it was particularly unusual for Dan Colter. In fact there was some criticism at a partners' meeting. Colter said he was not free to discuss the source or identity of Spartacus, and his partners had no choice but to respect his position.

Ronnie and I were both amazed at the side benefits of a hit record. In addition to everything else, Colter arranged for various merchandising rights. Toy companies, clothing manufacturers, ceramic companies, even linen manufacturers wanted to license the Spartacus name. They offered big advances, and a royalty percentage on every item sold. But there was something missing. A picture or visual representation was needed to put on the products. So Colter got Aben to have his art department create a Spartacus logo, using the same type as was on the album cover, and a drawing to go with it. They did a wild-looking rendition of a Roman gladiator with all the trappings, including a helmet, so that the face, half hidden, could be anybody. (Anybody except maybe Ronnie Finkelhof!) And the gladiator was playing guitar. He was in one of those typical rock musician singing poses. You know what I mean. They look like they're having a fit or something. Anyway, that solved the merchandising problem, and Colter must have made fifty deals. *More* money!

One of the most popular items was the Spartacus T-shirt. They sold by the millions. A lot of the kids at school wore them, especially the girls. The thing that was hard for Ronnie to bear was that Ginny wore one every day. She must have bought them by the dozen. Ginny was the Number One Spartacus fan in town, and everybody knew it. It was all she talked about. "I just *love* Spartacus," she said. What the silly broad didn't know was that Spartacus loved her!

I think that T-shirt had a lot to do with an incident that finally overheated Ronnie's libido. One evening we decided to go to The Apple, a disco that catered to teenagers. They had a tremendous sound system, and a disc jockey who played records so loud you could hardly talk. Everyone danced and just kind of mixed around. Ronnie and I had stopped in there once before, and he had wanted to leave within ten minutes. So I was surprised when he agreed to go again.

The place was packed, mostly with kids from our school. Ginny was there with Andy Hamilton. And she was wearing the Spartacus T-shirt as only she could wear it.

We sat in a corner booth, just drinking Cokes and watching. Ginny and Andy saw us, and, as I figured out later, decided to have some fun. They were looking our way and giggling and whispering to each other, and I thought it was just the usual "There's that drip Ronnie Finkelhof" routine again. But then they started coming over toward us. The two of them walked right up to our booth, and Ginny leaned over and said, "Hi, Ronnie." She didn't even acknowledge me. Ronnie jumped up and stammered something, and Ginny said, "I never see you here. Hope you're having fun." And with that they left, Ginny, as always, wiggling her tight blue-jeaned body across the floor.

Ronnie looked at me with a puzzled expression. "What do you suppose she did that for?" he asked.

"Damned if I know," I answered. I had figured maybe Ginny and Andy thought it was fun just to lead Ronnie on a little. Unfortunately, it was more devious than that. And cruel.

I realized later that Andy must have managed to drop something in Ronnie's Coke without our seeing him. What it was we'll never know—I'm not into drugs, and, of course, Ronnie wasn't either. But I'm sure it couldn't have been LSD or angel dust, or anything dangerous. It might have been pot like they put in brownies, or maybe amphetamines or some kind of upper. Whatever it was, Ronnie reacted fast. He got very animated, talked a mile a minute, and didn't make a real lot of sense. I'd never seen him like that, and it was a while before I began to suspect what had happened.

Then a Spartacus record came over the amplifying system. That did it! Between hearing his own record, the effect of the drug, and the sight of Ginny's body pressing against her T-shirt . . . *his* T-shirt . . . Ronnie let go of every inhibition. "I'm gonna ask Ginny to dance," he announced to me, and before I could react from the shock, he was up and walking across the floor. I could see that Ginny and Andy saw him coming, but they pretended they didn't until he was on top of them. I couldn't hear from where I was, but I saw Ronnie speak to Ginny.

She turned to Andy, and they both had impish grins on their faces. Andy nodded—it was clear he was encouraging her to accept. Then Ginny got up and they went out on the dance floor together.

The Spartacus record was still on. It was a slow number, and Ronnie managed not to look too bad, mostly by rocking back and forth with the music. He had Ginny in his arms and was holding her close. I couldn't believe my eyes. Then the song ended. I saw Andy talking to the disc jockey, and knew something was up. Suddenly, on came the loudest, hardest rock record they had. The dance floor exploded with kids doing their thing, and doing it well. Ginny started to boogie, and she was good. I couldn't believe Ronnie would try to keep up with her. But he was not to be outdone, and he broke into the most outlandish, pathetic movements you could imagine. There was Ginny, dancing up a storm, and Ronnie opposite her looking like a stupid ape. I have to say it. I wanted to die for him. But there was nothing I could do.

Naturally the two started attracting attention. Ginny gave everyone a sly wink. Then Andy got on the floor, and started to corral all the other dancers around Ronnie and Ginny. Pretty soon everyone else stopped dancing, and formed a circle around the two of them, like it was some fancy exhibition. They were all laughing, but Andy shushed them so that Ronnie wouldn't catch on. But Ronnie was oblivious. Ginny played it to the hilt, and Ronnie, completely high by now, just got wilder and more ridiculous in his gyrations. I couldn't watch. Those bastards, Ginny and Andy!

Mercifully the record finally came to an end. Ginny gave Ronnie a big kiss, right on the mouth, and said, ''Thanks, Ronnie, you're great,'' and walked back to her table with Andy. The whole place broke into applause, intermixed with muffled laughter, and they all went back to their tables. Ronnie was left standing in the middle of the floor, alone and confused. I jumped up, grabbed his arm, and led him back to our booth. He looked lost. I think he was coming down from the high, and wasn't quite sure what had happened.

"I feel a little sick," he said—and then he *was* sick, all over the floor. I grabbed him under the arms and hustled him out of there. Everyone was watching. When we got outside he heaved some more, a lot of it down his shirt front. He looked green, and I was beginning to get worried. Finally he stopped, and sat down right on the cement parking lot.

I managed to get him up and walking. It was a long way back to his house. We finally made it with his arm over my shoulder and mine around his waist. Fortunately his folks had gone to bed, so we were able to get up to his room without seeing anyone. I offered to help Ronnie with his things, but he said he could manage okay.

There was some of his puke on me, too, so I was glad to take off and get home myself.

CHAPTER

14

The next day Ronnie was very quiet on the way to school. Finally he said, "I made a fool of myself last night, didn't I?" How could I answer him? I didn't want to make him feel any worse than he did, but at the same time I felt maybe he should face up to a few facts of life.

"Look, Ronnie," I said, "I think Andy and Ginny put some kind of upper in your Coke last night."

"What do you mean?"

"Remember when they came over to our booth? I think Andy did it while we were looking at Ginny. You acted like I never saw you act before. And then getting sick and all. That *must* have been it."

Ronnie didn't answer. He just looked very somber.

"Why don't you forget Ginny? She belongs with a schmuck like Andy. She's not good enough for you." I was trying to get through to him, but Ronnie just kept walking, with this strange look on his face. That experience sure hadn't helped his ego any. Ronnie felt the fool of all time. He knew he must have looked like an idiot out on that dance floor, and he couldn't get it out of his head. And then, on top of it, to barf in front of everyone!

"Sam," Ronnie finally said, "I'd tell you you're my best friend, but since you're my *only* friend, I guess that doesn't mean much to you."

I didn't say anything, and we kept walking.

"But I want you to know something. You took care of me last night. You stood by me, and I'll never forget it. *Never.*"

"Ronnie, any buddy would have done the same."

"I don't think so. Being there for me puts you in *my* league with the kids, and that ain't good. You could make other friends if you wanted. I don't know why you put up with me. I really don't." Ronnie was close to tears.

I was embarrassed for him, and didn't know how to answer. And I didn't feel so noble either. He seemed to forget that I had my own social limitations. But the truth is, I wouldn't have traded my friendship with Ronnie for *anyone* in that stupid school.

We walked along in silence for a while, and then I said, "Look, Ronnie, that's what friends are for. Now knock off the gooey talk and forget last night. Pretend it never happened."

"Oh no, Sam. It happened all right. And I'm gonna do something about it."

"Like what?" I couldn't imagine.

"No one will ever do that to me again. Ginny, Andy, nobody!"

"What's on your mind, Ron?" I had never heard that tone of voice from him before.

"I'm coming out. I've decided. No more Mr. Loser. I'm gonna be Spartacus like I should have been in the first place."

"You serious?"

"You bet your ass I am! I'll work things out with my father first, and then we'll have a press conference, and do the whole thing. Goddammit, I've had it! We're calling Aben right after school and putting an end to this crap. He'll be delighted." Ronnie really had his back up. Frustrations had been building, and last night did it.

But surprise. Aben was *not* delighted. "Oh no, Ronnie," he said. "You can't do that now. There's an old saying in show business: 'Don't fool around with success.' "

"What do you mean?" Ronnie was really taken aback.

"This 'mystery man' gimmick is good. We can't take a chance that identifying you will burst the bubble. It's working too well. You've got to live with it now."

"For how long?"

"Until it's been milked. Until it's past its peak and can't be sustained any longer."

"Then what?"

"Then we have a big campaign where you come out of hiding—a whole new shot in the arm. But not now."

"When?" Ronnie felt miserable.

"It's hard to say," Aben answered. "Maybe years. The longer the better. Make it pay off as long as possible before we change the whole chemistry of the act and take a chance on the new image."

"But Aben—"

"Ronnie, trust me, Believe me, I know what's best. Let's worry about the next album. I'm going to need it soon. The first one will peak in the next month, and I want to be ready. Let's figure on a session a week from Saturday—that okay?"

"Well, yeah, Aben. But are you sure—"

"Ronnie, I'm sure. Now hang in there, kid. I know it must be getting to you, but the time will come—"

"Okay, Aben. I'll get the cassettes to you this week."

"Great, kid. See you then."

"Sure. G'bye, Aben."

Ronnie wasn't happy. "That Aben," he said to me. "It's all money with him. But what can I do? I can't go back on him now."

At the same time, deep down, Ronnie heaved a sigh of relief. At least he didn't have to face up to his father yet. And he still really wasn't ready to handle being exposed to the public. His feelings were mixed, to say the least.

In the meantime, Debbie was getting out of control. She was having a terrible time keeping such a delicious secret. If Aben was going to carry on with this game much longer, Debbie would have to be squelched. So Ronnie made a desperate move. He went into Debbie's room when she wasn't home, and found her diary. It had a lock on it, and he figured there were things written there that were very, very personal. He didn't try to open it—he just hid it where she could never find it.

When Debbie came home, Ronnie told her. She went crazy. "Did you open it?" she screamed. "Did you break the lock?" She was frantic.

"No," Ronnie said.

"Give it back. Give it back this instant." Debbie was very upset.

"Cool down, Debbie," Ronnie said. "I promise not to open it . . ."

"Then give it back," Debbie screamed.

" . . . on one condition," Ronnie went on.

"What? What!!??"

"That you keep our secret. That you tell *no* one that I am Spartacus."

"I won't, I won't! I *told* you I won't! I promise. Now give it back."

"I will, Debbie. But in good time. When it doesn't matter anymore. Meanwhile, it stays with me."

"That's blackmail! You can't do that. It's blackmail!"

"Let's just call it insurance," Ronnie said.

When Ronnie told me the story, I said, "What do you suppose is in that diary? It must be a lulu."

"I don't know, Sam. I can't imagine."

"You think it's anything bad?" I seemed to be more curious than he was.

"Only to her, is my guess. Maybe she lifted a candy bar off a drugstore counter, or cribbed on an exam, or some other dumb thing."

"You think that's all?"

"Who knows? I guess it's possible she and some boy played doctor. You know, 'You show me yours and I'll show you mine.' " Ronnie laughed. "Anyway, I hope I never have to find out. Probably nothing as bad as she thinks in her adolescent mind. But I'm glad I did it. I feel more comfortable about her keeping quiet.''

Ronnie was right. Whatever was in that diary, it did the trick . . . for the time being at least.

CHAPTER

15

Ronnie was nervous about the next recording session. Not about the recording itself—he kind of looked forward to it by this time—but he was now going in as Spartacus. ''Don't worry,'' Aben had said, ''I've got it figured out.''

We went to the studio early as planned, and found Aben there with a ski mask and a big cowboy hat in his hands. You know those ski masks. They're like a stocking that fits over the whole face and head, with openings for the mouth and eyes. Even the nose is covered except for the very tip. When Ronnie put it on, he could have been anybody. Then with that wild-looking hat on top, the disguise was perfect. Funny thing. Ronnie liked the outfit. With nobody seeing his face he could be in his own world, and perfectly comfortable with himself.

The musicians had not been told it was a Spartacus session, and when they began straggling in and saw the ''masked stranger,'' there were a few snide remarks. But one of them, a black cat named Dodo Carter, really went for the outfit.

"Hey, crazy, man. I dig it. Gimme five." He held out his hand, palm up, and Ronnie went along and laid it on him. "You gonna do the whole gig that way?"

"Sure, man. That's my thing. Okay?" Ronnie was doing just fine.

Dodo let out a big whoop. He reminded me of Richard Pryor. "Hot damn, why didn't I think of that? You are one wild cat. Gimme five again." I think maybe ol' Dodo was high on something. Ronnie played along, but he seemed a little uncomfortable. Then another musician, a guitar player who had been watching all this, went up to the two of them.

"Come on, you guys, let's cut the crap. What's with the outfit, man?" he said to Ronnie.

At that point Aben moved in. "It's Spartacus, you dummies. Now I want no more smart cracks from any of you birds. And no one leaves this studio until the session is finished, or you never work for Jetstream Records again. I don't care if we're here all night. Any questions?"

"Okay, man. It's cool, it's cool," someone said.

The musicians were busy picking at their instruments within minutes after that, and nobody had much more to say. Musicians are musicians, and everything really *was* cool. When anyone talked to Ronnie, they just called him "man" like always, and they got so into the music that nobody thought anymore about who was behind the mask.

The first song went quickly. It was something Ronnie had written right after the episode with Ginny at The Apple—he called it "You Don't Know Me." The lyrics meant more to me than to anyone else because I knew what was behind it, and there were tears in my eyes by the time Ronnie finished the first chorus. I don't think they spent more than an hour on the song before both Aben and Ronnie said it was a "take."

Ronnie was really operating. I think it was the mask that helped. A good part of Ronnie's problem was his own image of himself, and with his face totally hidden he felt more comfortable. I asked him about it later, but he seemed embarrassed by the question.

The next number was a problem. It was meant to be an up-tempo song called "Rockin' My Baby," and Ronnie didn't mean "in a tree top." He was looking for more of a hard rock background, and the arranger had goofed. So Ronnie spent two hours working it over with the musicians. He set a rhythm pattern that was a real gas, and then led the musicians through a head arrangement that knocked me out. I could see that Aben was impressed, too, not only by the sound, but by Ronnie's expertise and ability, and his command of the whole situation. Ronnie with the mask on was a different Ronnie!

"Okay, Aben, let's go for a take," Ronnie finally said. The master was finished within an hour after that.

Three sides were done that night, and it was well past midnight when we finished. Aben had made it an evening session to avoid the day workers around the place, and he figured, between the mask and keeping the musicians in the studio, that he had covered all the bases. But he forgot one thing. There was a pay telephone in the men's room!

You have to remember how big Spartacus was at that point. He was news, big news. We never found out who, but somebody made a phone call. Maybe for a payoff, maybe for a friend, or maybe just out of mischief. Whoever it was, a reporter and his photographer were waiting outside, and as we came through the locked door of the studio, the flashbulbs went off.

Fortunately Ronnie's face was still covered, since the musicians were with us. But the reporter came at him before we knew what was happening. The crazy nut went for Ronnie's mask—he was going to tear it off. Aben got in between and gave him a hefty shove, and as the reporter reeled back, the flashbulbs went off again. The musicians stood around like a bunch of jerks, saying things like, "Hey, man, what's comin' off?" or other remarks just as dumb. I wasn't worried too much about the pictures because you couldn't see Ronnie's face, but it hit me very fast that *my* face might be a problem, since it could lead to Ronnie. So I pulled my coat up over my head. I would have liked to help Aben, but I felt covering up was more important. Besides, Aben was doing okay. The reporter was on the ground after Aben's second shove, but the photographer was still flashing away. Aben took care of that with a swipe that sent the camera flying. I don't think it will ever take pictures again.

"Okay, guys, head for the car," Aben shouted, and the three of us took off down the street. But the reporter was on his feet and right behind. The last thing I heard was Dodo Carter saying, "Hey, man, cool it, huh? I don't dig violence."

We jumped in Aben's car, Ronnie in the backseat and me in the front, with Aben at the wheel. He had this big Cadillac, and by pressing one button, all four of the doors locked at once. And just in time, because before he could get the car started, the reporter was trying to get in. Aben pulled away so fast the tires squealed. I thought we were safe, but when I looked out the back window, I saw the reporter and photographer getting into their own car.

"They're following us, Aben," I said.

"I know," he answered. "Don't worry. I'll lose them."

Well, I always said Aben had a lot of talents. But I didn't know driving was one of them. It was late, and the streets were not crowded, so there wasn't too much to get in our way. But I don't ever want to experience a ride like that again. Aben went around turns, I swear, on two wheels. He flew over the crest of one hill so fast that all four left the ground, and when the car landed, we hit the roof.

"Strap in, you guys," Aben yelled, and on he went.

"What if a cop stops us?" I said. "Ronnie looks like a bandit in that mask. We'll end up in jail for sure."

"We can't let that happen," Aben answered.

Just as he said that we heard the siren, and saw the red lights flashing behind us. A police car had pulled out from a side street, and was right on our tail. The reporter's car was getting farther and farther behind, but now we had a more serious problem.

I thought Aben would surely pull over, but he just tramped it all the harder. On top of that, the crazy idiot turned off his lights, I guess to make it difficult for them to follow. Also, they couldn't read his license plate that way.

Next thing a second police car joined the chase, and I knew the jig was up for sure. But Aben kept going like a maniac.

I turned around to look at Ronnie. He had pulled off his mask, and all the blood had left his face, he was that pale. The poor guy was hanging onto the strap on the side of the car with both hands. I can't say I was in much better shape.

"Aben. *Aben!* Please, Aben," I said. "Don't you think we better stop? Aben . . . ?"

But Aben just leaned over the wheel, gripping it tightly. As we came to a red light he barreled straight on through, narrowly missing some cross traffic which screeched to a stop, blocking the intersection. I didn't get too good a look because Aben kept right on going, but the squealing of tires and crunch of metal behind us left no doubt as to what happened.

Then Aben slowed down, turned on his lights, and leisurely drove us home. That crazy Aben . . . I guess protecting his investment was worth the risk to him. But not to me . . . and not to Ronnie. Ronnie was very upset.

"Aben," he said when we were dropped off, "I don't think I can take much more of this. I'm sorry, it's getting out of hand. You've got to do something."

"You're right, kid." Aben looked concerned himself. "Those pictures will be on the front page tomorrow, and the press is going to give us a hard time for sure. One thing they don't like is to have their reporters messed up. And they don't like one paper having a scoop, either!"

"Can't we come out now?" Ronnie asked.

"Not yet. It's too early. Please, Ronnie, don't worry. This won't happen again. I'll think of something to cool down the media."

It was another sleepless night for Ronnie. And for me, too.

CHAPTER

16

Aben was right. We were all on the front page of the *Sun Times* the next morning. It was a great action shot. Ronnie was standing there in kind of an awkward pose, I had my coat pulled up over my head, and Aben, with his back to the camera, was shoving the reporter who was toppling backward halfway to the ground. One good thing: not one of our faces could be seen.

WHICH ONE IS SPARTACUS? the headline said. Then the story went on to tell how this enterprising reporter had discovered where Spartacus was recording, and had gotten this shot as they were leaving the studio. "Is Spartacus black or white?" the article went on to ask. Even though my face was covered, they could see my hands. They figured the guy in the mask was maybe a blind, or a "beard" as they say.

At school the story and picture were all anyone talked about. There was much discussion about which one of the two in the picture was Spartacus. Ginny, natch, said, "He's white. He *must* be!" No way could her dreamboat be anything like the likes of me!

But that story in the *Sun Times* was just the beginning. The press was out to get us, like Aben had said. It was no big deal that Spartacus might be black, but one writer

came up with a serious speculation. It was just a week
after the incident that he ran a piece in his nationally
syndicated column:

> This reporter has an idea why Jetstream Records is
> keeping Spartacus under wraps. Black or white, I
> think our teenagers' national hero might well be some
> kind of drug freak they don't dare expose. He may be
> so doped up that they have to keep him locked away
> while they feed his habit. How about it, Aben, do you
> dare let us meet him?

That was bad. It was picked up by all the media, and
the pressure on Aben was tremendous. Ronnie was very
upset, too. Ronnie Finkelhof a drug freak? Freaked out
is more like it.

Aben was closely watched by now, and we didn't dare
meet him or be seen together. So we talked mostly on
the telephone. First thing was to get the second album
finished. Aben had to arrange for a whole new studio,
because the old one was now staked out by kids half the
time. He even got new musicians who were not told it
was a Spartacus session. Somehow, three different stu-
dios later, and after much gumshoeing around, the album
got completed. In spite of all the turmoil, I have to tell
you the record was a killer. Better than the first, if that's
possible. Aben was ecstatic. Then he came up with a
shocker.

"You've got to make an appearance, Ronnie. This
dope thing is bad news. We have to show the world that
you're a totally straight cat before we get a serious backlash."

"You mean I'm coming out?" Ronnie asked. He was
both excited and yet somehow scared.

"You're going on television, young man. We'll cover the country—I mean the world—in one night!"

"*Television*???" Now Ronnie was more scared than excited. He had figured on just an announcement. But television! "I don't know if I can handle that, Aben. I think maybe—"

"What's the big deal, Ronnie? If you can function in a recording studio, you can do it in a television studio. You'll still have your mask on, and—"

"My mask? I thought you meant—"

"Sure, your mask. We're not coming out yet. I figure we get you on one of the top news shows for an interview, just to set everyone straight that you're no drug freak or anything."

"You mean I just have to talk . . . and with my mask on?"

"Sure. No big deal. And it should do the trick. Quiet things down for a while. What do you say, Ronnie?"

Ronnie didn't answer. Finally he said, "Okay, Aben. But I want it to be on the news. With Barbara Walters."

"Barbara Walters? Why not? That is, if I can get her to do an interview on the ABC news one night."

Ronnie had picked Walters for a reason. Ronnie told me, "Barbara Walters is my dad's favorite."

"I don't get it. What if your father recognizes your voice?"

"I'm gonna tell him. I just plain can't hide it anymore. The longer it goes on, the worse it will be when he finally finds out. Mom, too, but Dad in particular. You know what he's like."

"How you gonna handle it?"

"I'm not sure yet. Depends on how he reacts. Maybe I'll come off good, and he'll say, 'Hey, that's a bright young man.' "

"You think it'll go that way?"

"No. I'm just dreaming."

"Then what's the point of telling him after the show?"

"I don't know. I guess it's just that he has this great admiration for Walters, and if he sees me with her, maybe he won't put Spartacus down . . . and that might be the best time to hit him with the news. Maybe Walters will talk about me being 'young America's poet,' like *Newsweek* did. I guess what I'm really hoping is for Dad to *respect* Spartacus . . . just for a minute . . . long enough to make it easier for him to accept *me* that way—me, his ill-begotten son." Ronnie let out a nervous laugh. "What do you think?"

"I don't know, Ron. You'll just have to play it by ear."

Aben had no trouble setting the date with Walters. He could have made any deal he wanted with any network, but he handled it as a nonpaid, pure news shot. Walters agreed to the special appearance, but insisted on one thing.

"He's got to sing at least a song on the show," she said.

"Why?" Aben asked. "This isn't a performance. This is a news spot. I told you why we're doing this."

"I understand," Walters said, "and that's fine with me. But there's one problem. How will we know the man behind the mask is really Spartacus? You could have *anybody* do that interview, and the real Spartacus could be holed up in a room somewhere with a needle in his arm."

"Come on, Barbara, you don't really believe those silly rumors, do you?"

"It doesn't matter what I believe, Aben. It's what's been printed, and what the public thinks. I trust you, but I can't take the risk, however small, that this will turn out to be any kind of a hoax. He sings a song, or it's no deal.''

"Let me talk to Spartacus. I'll get back to you."

Well, Ronnie didn't like the idea too much. But as he thought about it, he figured he could do one of his more middle-of-the-road songs that his father might like. And with the mask on, he felt he would be okay. So the date was set.

Aben arranged for the interview to be taped at the studio late at night, and with great security. Ronnie handled himself beautifully. Walters caught on to his brightness very fast, and didn't try to make him look bad or distort the interview in any way.

"I notice you are talking strangely, Spartacus," Barbara Walters said after the introduction. "Is that your normal voice?"

"No," Ronnie answered. "I'm afraid some people close to me would recognize my voice. So if you'll forgive me, I prefer to talk in this manner." Ronnie had lowered his pitch to almost a growl—I would never have recognized him.

"Why are you hiding your true identity?" was the next question.

"I have a private life," Ronnie answered. "You must know, Ms. Walters, that I could not live a normal existence if my face and identity were known to the public."

"But wouldn't you like the prominence, the fame? Wouldn't you enjoy being a celebrity?"

"I suppose there are certain aspects of it that would make my life more interesting and exciting. But they're not worth the negatives. I'm only in high school now. I plan to go to college next year. I want to enter like other freshmen. I want the opportunity to live a normal life, with normal experiences, like *any* young student. Anonymity can be a great blessing, and I mean to keep it that way."

"How do you feel about the charges that you are on drugs, and that you are being kept from the public to hide your true image?"

"I feel bad about it. I would like young people, in particular, to know that music and drugs need have no relationship. That's why I'm here on your show. I hope you can recognize, through my mask, that I am totally straight. In fact, I must tell you that I have never even smoked pot, let alone indulged in the other, more serious drugs."

"Having talked with you at length before this taping, and being impressed with your obvious sincerity, I accept your word on that. But one more very important point. How do we know that *you* are Spartacus? How do we know that you are not a substitute sent in to hoodwink the public? Will you take off your mask now and identify yourself?"

"No, Ms. Walters. You know I'm not prepared to do that."

"Then, Spartacus, I will ask that you sing and play something for us. If you do, there can be no question that you are the young man himself."

"Of course."

Ronnie reached for his guitar, and did one of his most beautiful numbers. It was from his second album that was about to be released, and became a plug for the record. Aben had that figured as well. It was called "What Am I to Be?"

When the song finished, Walters said, "I think no one has any doubt now that you are Spartacus, and that you are everything you say you are. I thank you for making this appearance, and I, for one, understand your position, and reasons for staying anonymous. My best wishes to you for a happy and normal life.''

"Thank you," Ronnie said.

And that's the way it was. The show did everything it was meant to do when it went on the air the next evening—that is, everything it was meant to do for the public.

At Ronnie's house, things didn't go quite the way he had hoped.

CHAPTER

17

On the night of the airing, Mr. Finkelhof was at his favorite chair in front of the TV set. Ronnie, and occasionally Debbie, often watched the news with him, as did Mrs. Finkelhof. Ronnie had primed Debbie to let him handle things and not interrupt when he told his parents after the show. It was not easy to hold her down! Mr. Finkelhof had on his slippers, and was sipping a bourbon and water—his one and only of the day.

The top of the news was like every night. The economy, excerpts from a press conference the president had held that afternoon in Washington, a bomb explosion in England—nothing new. Ronnie was squirming in his chair, and Debbie was giving him knowing grins. Spartacus's appearance on the show had been well publicized so the program would get a top rating that night. I guess

the network wanted to hold the audience, because they
didn't get to the Spartacus interview until the very last.
Ms. Walters came on looking serious, yet with a slight
smile on her face.

"We have a unique story to explore tonight," she said.
"One of the most unusual happenings in what is, in itself, an unusual business, is the worldwide explosion on
the musical scene of a young man we know only as
'Spartacus.' I am sorry that we could not arrange to have
Spartacus live in the studio with us tonight due to security reasons. And I am sorry that the crowds that I understand have formed outside the studio will be
disappointed. However, last night I did have Spartacus
at another studio in another city, and I talked with him
at length. I did not see his face, however. He wore a
complete stocking mask, so that I have no more idea of
what he looks like than you will when I play you the
videotape of the interview we had on camera.

"First, I must tell you that I have the sworn statement
of perhaps the only person who knows the real identity
of Spartacus, the president of Jetstream Records, testi-
fying that the young man you are about to see is truly
that person. If there are still any doubts in your minds,
Spartacus will identify himself as only he can. Now . . .
please stand by." Walters was making the most of this
dramatic moment!

Old Mr. Finkelhof kind of snorted at that point, Ronnie told me, which didn't help the mood any. But after
that, he sat and watched quietly during the whole interview. I was, of course, watching it at home, and Ronnie
really did come off great. He was bright, articulate, and
you had to believe him and know he was sincere and
totally straight. Unfortunately, Mr. Finkelhof didn't see
it that way.

"That's the most obvious hoax I have ever witnessed," he said when the show was over.

"Why, Dad?" Ronnie asked, almost pleadingly.

"It's an out-and-out promotion. The whole thing is nothing but a publicity stunt. You don't believe for one minute that ridiculous story has an ounce of validity to it, do you? I'm embarrassed that our firm represents the people involved, and I intend to tell Dan Colter so tomorrow. Furthermore, I'll wager that not one of Spartacus's songs would have seen the light of day without all this nonsense. Do you young people really consider what he does music?"

"But Daddy, Spartacus's first song was a big hit before any of this started," Debbie blurted out. It was the wrong thing to bring up.

" 'I'm Gonna Romance the Pants Off of You'? You call that a song? If that's what it takes to have a hit, I'm sorry about the whole younger generation. It's disgraceful!"

In spite of Ronnie's glare, Debbie kept on. "Daddy, you don't understand. Spartacus is super. He's a poet. *Everybody* loves his music."

At that point Mrs. Finkelhof had her own comment to make. "Why all the fuss about Spartacus? I'm sure tomorrow there will be a new teenage hero to take his place. You young people are very fickle, you know. Anyway, it's none of our concern."

Ronnie was struggling with a decision. He had hoped to tell his folks that night. But it was not working out the way he figured. Then his father cinched it.

"Well," said Mr. Finkelhof, "all I can say is, I'm glad he's not *my* son."

Ronnie went to his room.

CHAPTER

18

The next day the regular weekly partners' meeting was held at Mitchell, Payne, Dillingham, Colter and Finkelhof. Before the scheduled business was brought up, Mr. Finkelhof had a lot to say. "Did any of you see that Spartacus interview on the news last night?" There was a chorus of yeses.

"Dan," said Mr. Finkelhof, "I think you should tell the partners of this firm something about who and what we are dealing with. This whole promotion has a smell to it that disturbs me, and I am concerned that Mitchell, Payne could find itself representing a person, or group of persons, of an unsavory background. This isn't the kind of client we have ever solicited in the past, and I, for one, don't understand why we are involved in such a situation now."

"Ben," Colter answered, "I fully understand your position and your concern. And I must apologize to all the partners for not being totally open about the background of my client. But you must respect the fact that I am committed to secrecy."

"If you must represent him," one of the partners said, "why, may I ask, are you doing so at an hourly rate? For assuming total legal and fiscal responsibility, let alone the investment success you've had, it's certainly worth a percentage—say five percent—if not more. At least have the firm fully benefit from the Spartacus bonanza."

Another partner cut in. "Dan, we know the Spartacus trust is close to thirty million, and that's only the beginning. You are acting as trustee, and are directly responsible for the enhancement of Spartacus's earnings. It would not be uncommon for an entertainment-oriented firm to take even *ten* percent of his income. We could be talking about huge fees here."

"Please, gentlemen," Colter said, "you will have to—"

Mr. Finkelhof interrupted. "Hold on, Dan. I am more concerned with what this is doing to our firm than what we could be making from it. You know our primary client base is corporate. The publicity we are getting is interfering with normal business. Our switchboard is overloaded, and the kind of characters that show up in our reception room looking for Spartacus is most disturbing. One of my clients has even criticized what he calls our 'getting into show business.' "

"Gentlemen, gentlemen, please—" Colter was at a loss as to how to respond.

Another partner interrupted. "Just a minute. It's true we *are* inconvenienced by this Spartacus situation, and for the amount of money we are getting, we might well question whether it pays to continue with this representation. On the other hand, everything has its price, and I am certain there is a point of compensation that will make it worthwhile to all of us. And certainly to you, Dan." There was a murmur of agreement from the room. "What do you say?"

Colter was silent. Finally, he said, "First of all, I must

tell you that I cannot change the fee structure—at least not at this time."

"But, Dan—"

"Please, gentlemen, let me finish. Even if the client were to agree, there is another problem, a personal one, that unfortunately I am not free to discuss. You must simply accept the fact that I can *not* in good conscience charge more than what is the accepted minimum for a case of this kind. Nor can I consider the alternative of giving up representation entirely. I *do* understand the position of the partners. But the best I can promise right now is that I will take up the matter with my client. For reasons that I am not in a position to tell you, he is the only one who can resolve this situation. I am sorry. There is no more I can say."

The room was quiet. Finally the senior partner broke the silence. "The Spartacus matter is tabled for now." And they went on to the next order of business.

The following day Colter gave Ronnie a complete rundown of the partners' meeting.

"I have a problem, Ronnie. You have put me in an untenable position."

"I'm sorry, Mr. Colter. What do you want me to do?"

"Tell your father everything. It's the only solution. No one else if you insist, but at least your father. That way we could come to an arrangement. Besides, I can't look him in the eye anymore."

"I've tried, Mr. Colter. But you know his opinion of Spartacus and the whole publicity thing. I don't know how he'll take it. It's gone too far. I should have told him what I was doing in the first place. Then it wouldn't be so bad. But now . . ."

"I understand, Ronnie. But it can only get worse the

longer you wait. One thing is for sure. It won't get better."

"Please, Mr. Colter. Give me some time. I just need the right moment."

"And what do I tell my partners in the meantime?"

"I don't know. Do you want me to get another lawyer? I'll release you if that will help."

"Ronnie, how can I do that? I did accept your confidence, God help me. How can I send you off to a stranger who will be certain to exploit you one way or another? No, I can't do that."

"Then raise your fees like they want. Take a percentage of my income. That should satisfy them."

"And your father? How will he feel when he learns the truth? He shares in those fees, you know. I just can't do that without his knowledge. It's contrary to my moral, fiscal, and perhaps even legal responsibilities. Ronnie, until at least your father is aware of all the facts, I am afraid I am stuck with a dilemma."

"But, Mr. Colter—"

"No, Ronnie. The more I think about it, the more I know that there is nothing I can do but tell my partners that everything is status quo."

"I'm sorry, Mr. Colter. I don't know what to say. Is there *anything* I can do?"

"Only one thing, Ronnie. Tell your father . . . tell him as soon as possible."

"I'll try, Mr. Colter. I really will. Just give me a little more time."

The meeting broke up with neither Ronnie nor Colter very pleased with the outcome.

CHAPTER

19

A lot of other things were happening about this time. For one, a musician from the very first session surfaced. He, of course, had seen Ronnie without his mask, and when he heard the records later, he talked around about it. "I seen that cat Spartacus," he said. Word soon got to the press, and for about a week he was big news, sought out by every talk show in the business. But it didn't last long.

Merv Griffin had him on first. The guy's name was Skeets Gallagher; he was the drummer on that first session. I don't know about most drummers, but this one was pretty much out of it. I remember him well—how could I forget! I wouldn't necessarily say he was "punk," but he did look a little weird. He had this long hair, which wasn't so unusual, except he had it tied in a knot on top of his head. Then he was wearing one of those tank shirts, and real tight pants made of kind of a black shiny material. On second thought, maybe he *was* a real punker. Anyway, he was a character. But I'll say this: he sure could play drums.

Ronnie and I watched the show together. Skeets was dressed pretty much the same as before when he walked out on the stage and sat down next to Merv.

"Mr. Gallagher, I understand you were the drummer on Spartacus's first session," Merv opened up.

"Yeah, I did that gig."

"Can you tell us what Spartacus looks like?"

"Well, yeah, I guess so. He was . . . he was . . . well, it was some time ago. And you see, he was sittin' in this isolation booth, and, well, man, I wasn't like payin' too much attention to him. No way did I know he was going to be . . . well, was . . . Spartacus."

"But certainly you remember *something* about him. First of all, was he black or white?"

"Hey, man, you know that don't make no difference to me. I figure we're all the same."

"Of course, but surely—"

"It's the music a cat blows that counts. That's all I care—"

"Mr. Gallagher—"

"Skeets. Just call me Skeets, man."

"Skeets. I can't believe you don't remember if he was black or white. I would think—"

"He was white. Yeah, I'm sure. He was a white cat."

"Fine. Now, can you tell us, was he blond or brunet?"

"Whatsat?"

"Did he have dark or light hair?"

"Uh, I ain't so sure. I think it was kind of in the middle."

"Was he tall or short?"

"Uh, I think he was . . . uh . . . I'd say about medium height. Yeah, he was like medium."

"Was he fat, or thin? Or—I'm afraid to ask—average weight?"

"Yeah, you got it. Like average weight."

"I see. Well, Skeets—"

"But that cat could really do his thing. He played a mean guitar, and he had a set of pipes that turned me on."

"Yes, we all know about that, Skeets, and I want to thank you—"

"And his songs, man—they're outrageous!"

"Yes. Thank you, Skeets Gallagher, drummer on the first Spartacus session. One of the few people ever to see the face of Spartacus." At that point the camera moved in on Merv and cut Skeets out of the picture. "Now that we all know what Spartacus looks like," Merv said to the audience, "I am sure (ahem) that you'll be able to spot him if he shows his face on the street! And now, this message . . ."

Ol' Merv had this funny smile on his face, and he did not bring Skeets back after the commercial. Skeets did make one more talk show, but the others who had booked him canceled.

Another musician surfaced after that, a guitar player, but he wasn't much more help than Skeets. As for the engineer, Aben told us not to worry about him. Aben apparently paid him a lot of money for each session, and the kid knew where his loyalties lay—or you might say where he got his bread. Anyway, the worst he could do would be to give a description.

We had been watching the *Merv Griffin Show* at Ronnie's house, and since it was late in the afternoon, Ronnie's mom asked me if I'd like to stay for dinner. That was the first time she had ever done that, and I looked at Ronnie.

"Yeah, Sam, stay. We're having fried chicken, turnip greens, and black-eyed peas," Ronnie said. It was the kind of joke we made between us, like blacks will make with each other. Ronnie and I were easy that way. But his mother didn't get it.

"Ronnie!" his mother cut in. "What are you talking about? We're having nothing of the kind. I have a beautiful rack of lamb in the oven, with roast potatoes, and—"

"Never mind, Mom, I was only kidding," Ronnie said. We both laughed. Anyway, I stayed.

The evening was an interesting experience for me, because it was the first time I had ever been exposed to Ronnie's father for more than a quick "hello." Ronnie's sister, Debbie, had been invited to a friend's house, so there were just the four of us.

"I understand you are a senior in high school, too," Mr. Finkelhof said to me at dinner.

"Yes, sir."

"What do you plan to do after graduation? Will you be able to go to college?"

"Well, I'm going to work this summer. And then I hope to go to State. I've applied for financial aid, but I won't know for another month or two."

"Ronnie, you know, has received early acceptance to Harvard," Mr. Finkelhof said proudly. I glanced at Ronnie. He hadn't told me. "I'm looking forward to his going to law school there, too. Eventually he will join our firm and keep the name Finkelhof in the title long after I retire. Have you ever thought about the law, Sam?"

"Well, not really, sir. That's a little far ahead for me to think right now."

"You should think about it, young man. The law is what our whole society is based on. It's the key to our civilization. It's what sets us apart from primitive man. Without it we would be not much more than savages."

"Yes, sir." I didn't know what else to say, and Ronnie had his face in his plate.

"The American system of jurisprudence is the only bulwark we have against total chaos. I know that the problem of crime and disorder in our country is far from solved, but I feel that is more a function of our educational system than anything else."

"I'm sure you're right, sir."

"It's our younger generation that needs guidance and counsel. Their morals have totally disintegrated, and it's evidenced in everything. Take your popular music, for instance." Ronnie was deeper in his plate than ever, and I was beginning to squirm. "The lyrics have innuendos of sex, drugs, and what have you. I know Ronnie has no use for today's music, and I hope you feel the same."

"I agree, sir." It seemed the only thing to say, and I wanted to get him off the subject. Ronnie shot me a glance.

"Well, I'm glad to hear that. I'm sure you are aware that our firm represents Spartacus. It is a constant source of embarrassment to me. For some crazy reason my friend and partner, Dan Colter, accepted him as a client, but I can assure you somehow I'll put an end to that." Then he turned to Ronnie. "I meant to tell you, Ronnie, the partners had a long discussion on the Spartacus matter, and we expect to have it resolved at our next meeting."

"Ben," Mrs. Finkelhof finally cut him off, "let the boys alone with your preaching and eat your dinner. We're having a delicious apple pie for dessert, so finish up."

"No watermelon?" I asked. I couldn't resist trying to lighten things, but they just looked at me funny. They still didn't get it. But I got it. Finally I began to better understand Ronnie's problem about telling his father. It had gone too far. It would embarrass Mr. Finkelhof terribly among his partners, as well as everyone in the community who knew him. I talked with Ronnie about it later.

"Ronnie, maybe you should *never* come out."

"What're you talkin' about, Sam?"

"You have to make a decision at some point. Maybe you should quit right now. Forget Spartacus. Don't make any more records. You have all the money you'll ever need. End it. No one will ever know. Maybe some day when you're a big, successful attorney you can tell the whole story. Anyway, how can you go to college as Spartacus?" Ronnie looked at me funny at that point. "You *are* going to college, aren't you? And law school?" Then I got a surprise.

"I don't know, Sam."

That's the first inkling I got that Ronnie was possibly looking at music as his career. I hadn't figured that. But at the same time, I had noticed lately that Ronnie was coming out somewhat, coming out of himself, I mean. He was standing up a little straighter, and just seemed more at ease when there were other kids around. The way he would order a pizza from the waitress was no longer in that apologetic manner he usually had. I suppose I should have felt good about Ronnie beginning to show a little self-confidence. But for some reason, I didn't.

Strangely enough, it depressed me.

CHAPTER

20

Ronnie's new-found confidence unfortunately led to new frustrations. Like that day he saw Ginny eating alone in the school cafeteria, and decided he was going to join her.

"Okay if I sit down?"

"Well, yeah . . . I guess so . . . . " Ginny wasn't too happy about her lunch partner, and kept looking around to see if anyone was watching.

"How come Andy's not here today?" Ronnie asked.

"Well, if you must know, we had a fight."

"What about?"

"Nothing . . . nothing that would interest you."

The conversation wasn't going well, and Ronnie was beginning to wish he had never sat down with Ginny in the first place.

"Well, I'll tell you what about if you really want to know," Ginny finally said after an awkward silence. "He's jealous of Spartacus."

"Spartacus?"

"Yeah, Spartacus. You've heard of him, haven't you?" It was said in a slightly sarcastic way.

"How can he be jealous of Spartacus? You don't even know him."

"Of course not. But Andy thinks I play his records

too much. And he says I talk about him all the time. He thinks all of us girls are nuts because of how we feel about Spartacus.''

"You like Spartacus that much, Ginny?''

"I *love* him. I'd give anything to meet him. *Anything!*''

"But you don't even know what he looks like.''

"Sure I do. I know he's tall because of that picture in the paper. And with the songs he writes and that voice— well, he must be absolutely *beautiful.*''

"Well, I don't know if—''

"Look, Ronnie, I gotta run.'' Ronnie had hardly touched his food, while Ginny had finished hers very fast. "I have a meeting with my advisor,'' she said, and was on her feet and gone before Ronnie could say another word.

Ronnie picked me up later and told me the whole dumb story. Then as we were walking to class, there were Ginny and Andy, looking very cozy. She was standing right up against him, and you knew the fight was over. Neither of us commented. What was there to say?

Another thing that set Ronnie off happened in our psychology course. Mr. Dursch was one of those teachers who liked to relate our study to current events, and he decided to "take a look at the Spartacus phenomenon . . . the psychology of the reaction of youth to his music,'' as he put it. Then he began to analyze the Spartacus lyrics, and to tell us what they all meant.

I guess I knew better than anyone what was behind Ronnie's songs, and Dursch was so far off that it made me wonder about everything else he had been teaching us all year. Ronnie and I exchanged pained looks. Then Mr. Dursch got into the mask, and the secrecy part— and what was behind all that.

"I'm not going to give you my views now, " he said. "I have some definite thoughts, but first I want to hear yours. Your assignment, due in one week, is to write a five-hundred-word paper on Spartacus. You are to assume his identity—the man behind the image. The paper is to be written in the first person, describing why you have kept hidden, and what you, the real person, are really like. You have heard enough of Spartacus's lyrics, and you have all read enough about him. Let's see how each of us analyzes the real man from these various clues and manifestations. Class dismissed."

"What are you going to do?" I asked Ronnie on the way home.

"I'm gonna tell the truth," Ronnie said. "I'm gonna tell it like it is, and see if that dumb ass gets it."

"This could be very interesting," I said. "Veeeerrrrry interesting."

The papers were due in one week.

CHAPTER

21

I am unattractive, shy, introverted, and without friends, except for one. My friend is a loner, too, by reason of his own social handicap, and therefore offers me no entree to others . . .

Mr. Dursch was reading from one of the Spartacus papers. I looked over at Ronnie, and he nodded. It was his.

. . . When I say I am shy, that is an understatement. It is just not possible for me to relate to my peers, to be at ease with them, to engage in a normal high school life. Perhaps it is my looks, or at least my own image of my physical self. Perhaps it is the lack of a sibling with whom I could learn to relate. Perhaps it is my inherent clumsiness, my inability to engage in common sports activities with those who might have become my friends. Or perhaps it is my intellectual approach to class discussions, which seems to annoy my classmates and turn them away from me . . .

Ronnie told his whole story, changed only slightly where it might identify him. Mr. Dursch read key parts of the paper and then went to the last paragraph.

. . . I live between two impossible alternatives. I never expected to be such a big hit, and even if the decision to come out were mine, I don't know what I would do. It's a big problem for me, and I try not to think about it too much. Most of my fans are probably saying to themselves, "I'd like to have that kind of problem."
    Don't be too sure.

"I won't identify the writer," Mr. Dursch said, "but I must point out that this is totally contrary to how I see the real Spartacus. Now let me read you part of another paper with a completely different interpretation."

I am six feet tall and have a good physique. I grew up in Southern California and spent most of my spare hours on the beach. I am an expert surfer, and play a good game of tennis. At a very early age I knew that music was to be my career, and I hounded the record companies. I was certain I would be successful. Finally one agreed to give me a chance. But the president of the company said he didn't like my name, and

wanted some gimmick to exploit me, like a wild costume or crazy makeup. Then he hit on the mask and
mystery man idea. I hated it, but I wanted the deal,
so I signed a contract, agreeing not to disclose my
identity without his permission.

Ronnie and I exchanged glances. He was slowly shaking his head as Mr. Dursch went on.

As you know, I was every bit as successful as I knew
I would be. But not being able to openly live the role
of Spartacus is driving me crazy. I have an active
social life and all the girlfriends I want, but I can't
stop thinking of what it would be like to be famous.
I really love being with people, and want nothing
more than to take advantage of the success and glamour my talents have brought me.

"There's more," Mr. Dursch said, "but that will give
you the essence. I have no doubt that the person behind
Spartacus is everything this paper represents him to be—
an outgoing, attractive young man, sure of himself, with
a very strong ego. His lyrics may mislead you, but they
merely demonstrate sympathy for others less gifted, a
sense of guilt not uncommon in one who has everything.
This is a good illustration of 'compensating manifestations.' The image is perfect, and I congratulate the writer
for seeing him so accurately. It's the work, incidentally,
of Ginny Baker."

The papers were handed back after class. Ginny, of
course, got an A. I got a B—mine was a lot of junk
purposely far from the truth. Guess who got a D?

Ronnie was freaked. "My paper was right on the
nose," he said after class, "and look what that dimwit
gives me!"

"It probably won't affect your final grade that much." I said.

"That's not the point. It's the idea. Besides, word's gotten around that it was my paper he read, and everyone's having a big laugh. And Ginny, with her wild image of Spartacus, treats me like garbage—while she tells me she loves me—him, I mean. I'm—*he's* the idol of every kid in this school, and they all look at me as the class goon. You know something, Sam, I don't even *want* their stupid friendship. They're all miserable, snotty nerds as far as I'm concerned. But I'd like to show them— oh boy, how I'd like to show them. I'd like to let them *all* know who I am, and then tell them where to get off!'' Ronnie was really pissed.

"You think that's what you'd do?" I asked. I wasn't too sure.

Ronnie didn't answer. He was so caught up in his frustrations that he hardly said another word all the way home.

CHAPTER

22

"It shipped platinum," Aben screamed on the phone to me. That meant that on the second album the initial orders from the distributors were over a million copies. "On top of that, the reaction from the jockeys is fantastic. We don't know which single to put out

first. This album is going to be bigger than the first.''
Aben was really up.

"That's great, Aben. I'll tell Ronnie right away.''

"Have him call me. We've got to talk. There's something on the burner that can't wait. And it's hot.''

What he had on the burner was a network TV show. This wasn't another of the endless guest shot requests that came in every day. This was a special, starring Spartacus—prime time. And the money was big, Ronnie's own package. The offer was from NBC. I guess they were trying to make up for the Walters interview. Ronnie, Aben, and I met for lunch at a restaurant out on the highway where we wouldn't be likely to see anybody we knew.

"Negotiations have been going on for over a month,'' Aben said. "But I didn't want to get into it with you until it was right.''

"Gee, Aben, I don't know if—''

"Let me finish, Ronnie,'' Aben cut in. "The problem was they wanted you to appear bare-faced. Big brilliant idea! Network vice-presidents! Who needs them!''

"I don't understand, Aben. You want me to do a TV show with my mask *on*?''

"Of course. Two reasons. First, I know you can work that way. A TV special is a big deal, and I don't want to take any chances on your performance. There could be fifty million people watching.''

"Fifty million?!!''

"Easy—or more. So it's got to be good. And secondly, I'm not yet ready to blow the 'mystery man' label. It's still working for us.''

"Aben, fifty million people—I don't know . . .''

"Look, kid, you'll be in a studio, it will be taped, and with your mask on, everything will be cool. I'm certain of it. Also, I'm producing the show personally, and I guarantee you'll come off a big winner.''

"If I don't like something, can I tape it over?''

"Up to a point. Don't forget there will be a studio audience.''

"Oh, do we have to have an audience? Couldn't we—''

"Have to, Ronnie. Gotta have the reaction. And you'll perform better with people watching. You'll see. Now relax, and leave everything to me. All you have to do is show up and do your numbers. The production aspects and other parts of the show will be my problem.''

"When are we supposed to do this?''

"I arranged taping for a Saturday, eight weeks from now. You won't even have to attend rehearsals. We'll use musicians who have worked with you before, and you'll be doing your same record numbers. You can come in on Saturday morning for a dress, and Saturday evening we tape. It'll be a breeze.''

"Okay, Aben. I guess I can handle that.'' Ronnie was acting like it was no big deal, but inside his stomach was in a knot.

"Sure, I know you can handle it, kid.'' Aben went right on. "I'll meet with Colter and work out the whole package, production fees, all of it. We're both gonna make a bundle on this one. By the way, are you straight with Colter?''

"Not really. He's pressing me.''

"Can't you trust your father? I don't know him, but I would think he'd go along with you.''

"It's more than that, Aben. It's hard to explain, but I'm afraid now of what it would do to him—and our family. But I'll get to it. I have to. Anyway, don't worry about Colter. He will never go back on his word. Go ahead and meet with him.''

Ronnie and I caught the bus back to town.

CHAPTER

23

The next day Aben called. He had a lot of wild ideas about how Spartacus should dress for the show, but Ronnie kept turning them down. Finally they settled on blue jeans, boots, and a western-type shirt. No tank shirt, bare chest with a gold medal around the neck, or any other affectations. Ronnie was insistent, so Aben went along. "Next thing, Aben, you'll want me to dress like Liberace and have sequins on my mask," Ronnie said. "Hey, good idea, man," Aben answered. I think he meant it.

That eventful Saturday was on us very fast. The taping was set at NBC's affiliate station in Chicago, and it was no big deal for Ronnie to be away from home for the day and evening. He put on his blue jeans and shirt in the morning, and we headed for the city. A six-million-dollar star riding the bus to do his own show! NBC would have been happy to send a limousine, or a fleet of them to pick him up, but, of course, we couldn't do that.

Aben had told Ronnie to go to an address not too far from the NBC station. It turned out to be a private town house that he had rented. I was to leave Ronnie at that point, and go on to the studio alone. That kind of bugged me, but Aben felt I shouldn't be seen with him once he had on his mask and was Spartacus. Somebody who knew me might see us together. I suppose that made sense, but I couldn't help feeling put out. However, when we got to the house, Ronnie asked me not to leave yet, so I went inside with him and stuck around for a while. Aben was there and had Ronnie's mask and hat.

"How do we do this?" Ronnie asked.

"You mask up, get in my car, and lie low in the back while we drive to the studio. There it's all taken care of. They've got enough police to get the president of the United States in without any trouble."

"What about me?" I asked.

"You'll have to grab a cab, Sam. Here's a ticket to the show; you'll be in the audience. Sorry it has to be that way, but we can't take any chances."

"Sure, Aben, I understand."

It was about noon at that point, and Ronnie had to go to rehearsal. So I left and went out to get some lunch. Then I had the whole afternoon to waste before the taping, which was scheduled for 7:00 P.M. I thought of going to a movie, but I was too nervous. I also was in a funny mood, kind of lonesome and feeling out of it. I suppose Aben was right—that I shouldn't be around Ronnie when he was Spartacus. And yet I felt I was *part* of Spartacus. I had been there from the beginning. I was the support, the crutch that made it possible to happen. At least I *looked* at myself that way. Filled with mixed emotions, I walked aimlessly around town all afternoon.

Finally at about six o'clock I got a cab. I didn't know this side of Chicago that well, or I would have found a cheaper way to get to the studio. Crowds were all around the place, mostly teenagers. The taping had not been

publicized, but, of course, word got out. There were just
too many network people that knew about it. The kids
that had tickets were told only that it was a special, but
rumors were strong that it was a Spartacus show.

I hung around for a while outside, watching the action.
Ronnie must have been delivered through a back door
someplace, because no one had seen him, and some of
the kids had been there for hours. The cops were having
a rough time, and at one point it looked like the crowd
was going to break through.

I finally pushed my way inside. That ticket in my hand
was gold. I could have sold it a hundred times, and I
have to admit that the money being offered was tempting.
The cab ride coming over was the first one of my life,
and I really couldn't afford that kind of travel. But of
course, I kept my ticket—I had to see the show.

Inside there were more cops. And it was a good thing.
That audience was alive, and I mean alive. You never
saw such excitement. NBC pages were working hard trying to get them settled down. Finally a man walked out
on the stage and got the audience quiet. He told us they
wouldn't begin until there was order, and that did it.

"Ladies and gentlemen, welcome to NBC." He was
the emcee for the show. "The taping you will see tonight
will be aired a week from Tuesday at 9:00 P.M." There
were a few cheers. Then he told us about the applause
sign up above the stage, that we were to relax and have
a good time, laugh if we felt like it, applaud if we felt
like it, and all that. He told a few jokes, told us again to
enjoy ourselves, and started to walk off. Then he turned
back and said, "Oh, I almost forgot to tell you. The star
of our show tonight is . . . Spartacus!"

Well, I thought the roof was going to blow off. The
screams were so loud I had to hold my ears. The kids in

that audience went crazy. They were all standing and yelling and carrying on. It was the first time I had seen a group reaction to Spartacus. I knew he was big, but I was just not prepared for anything like this. The poor emcee had to get everyone's attention all over again. Finally a voice boomed out over a loudspeaker, "If order is not restored, the auditorium will be cleared, and the show will proceed without you." Things settled down again, the emcee gave us another warning, and finally the curtain opened and the show began.

First came a big production number. There was a huge chorus line of girls dressed in kind of Roman gladiator outfits. They had on very short skirts, and high-laced sandals on their feet. For brassieres they had these metal cups, but most everything else was bare. There were wide bracelets on their arms, and their heads were covered with gladiator masks—I guess something like Roman headgear—to symbolize the mask of Spartacus. You couldn't see their faces, but who cared.

There was a big orchestra, playing a medley of Ronnie's songs. I never heard his music arranged that way. It sounded like the pit band at a show, and I can't say I liked it too much. In the background was a huge cutout of the Spartacus logo, taken right from the cover of his first album. It was made of brass, or at least looked like it, and it picked up and reflected all of the colored lights. The dancing and music went on for about five minutes. Then they stopped for a commercial, which we watched on a television screen in the corner of the auditorium. While that was going on, men were resetting the stage for the next number. Then the emcee came out again. I don't remember his name, but I knew I had seen him as a host on one of those game shows. The audience was behaving fairly well at that point.

"And now, with no introduction necessary," the emcee said, "we are proud and privileged to bring you the young man who has taken this country by storm . . . the one you have all been waiting for. . . . Ladies and gentlemen . . . Spartacus!"

Over the last part the screaming had started again. I know when the show was aired that they cut down the audience mikes, but in the studio it was so noisy you could hardly hear anything. At that point Ronnie walked out on the stage, dressed in his blue jeans and western shirt, mask and hat fully in place. I thought the screams were loud before, but that was nothing compared to now. It was bedlam. There was no way to quiet the crowd, so the show proceeded anyway.

Ronnie stood there in front of the mike with his guitar, kind of half-bowing. There was no expression on his face, because there *was* no face. It was weird, I have to say. Finally he nodded to the group and went into his first number.

I've never understood why kids scream and yell so much at a concert. You'd think they'd shut up and listen to what they came to hear. There was a girl next to me who had huge tears running down her face, and she was gasping with sobs. I had never seen that kind of emotion—over *music*! A lot of the other kids were crying, and one girl, she must have been about fifteen, looked like she was having a fit. It scared me. What had little Debbie started when she sent in that tape? And what had Aben, Ronnie, and, I guess, me—what had we done?

The show was kind of a blur to me. Ronnie did three numbers in a row, not that anyone in the studio could hear them. After that there was a guest star, a comic that was just a stage wait as far as the kids were concerned. Then Ronnie came back to more screams and did two more songs. The show finished with another big production. The whole thing was over before I knew it.

I had told Ronnie and Aben that I would meet them back at the town house. It was another cab ride I couldn't afford, but I didn't know how else to get there. I waited an hour outside that place, but they never showed up. Maybe something went wrong. Or maybe they just plain forgot about me!

I finally left and found my way to the depot. I didn't expect too much more from Aben, but *damn* Ronnie! How could he leave me there like some lackey? Then I figured maybe they couldn't help it, that there must have been riots at the studio and they were trapped or something.

I rode home on the bus alone.

CHAPTER

24

I slept badly that night, and was anxious to see Ronnie the next day. He didn't bother to ask how I got home, but did say that they were stuck in the studio for hours because of the mobs. Which I suppose explained things. Still, he might have shown some interest in what happened to me. But I decided to put it out of my head. Maybe I was looking for a reason to feel sorry for myself. So I just asked Ronnie how he had finally gotten out of there.

"I took off my mask and hat and left."

"What?"

"First Aben and I changed shirts. Then I walked out the front door like anyone else, and met Aben at the car."

"Of course! Nobody would know you."

"It was funny. Everyone was jammed around the stage door. I stood in the middle of the mob for a while just to watch and listen. I even asked some kid how he liked Spartacus."

"Sorry I missed all the fun," I said. I couldn't resist the remark, but it passed over Ronnie's head. He was too much into himself—and the excitement of show biz. But I was beginning to feel bored with it all. Or was it something more than that? Truth is, I was feeling left out. My role in this whole caper was as a first-class stooge. Damn it, Ronnie, I thought, you wouldn't be where you are if it weren't for me. In a lot of ways! Or would he? I didn't know *where* I belonged in this picture, and I didn't like the feeling. But I kept it to myself.

As for Aben, he was living high. He had made a bundle as packager of the show. More important, the television exposure had caused a big jump in sales of Ronnie's records—not only the new album, but the first one again as well. For a small company like Jetstream, it was all gravy. With no increase in overhead, Aben was raking it in. He could have sold his company at that point for fifty to a hundred million dollars easy, and retired. But Aben was a real pro. He loved the business, and although he enjoyed the money, the power base was more important. Spartacus gave him that. Not only did he control the records, but in a sense he was the artist himself. No one could get to Spartacus to try and steal him, make a deal, manage him, or even get a story for a fan magazine. Colter was no help to anyone: Since the law firm had set up procedures to bar visitors in regard to Spartacus business, everything had to be done by mail. There was only Aben to talk to, and he loved it. Reminds me of Colonel Parker and Elvis, only more so.

They say power corrupts. But Aben seemed to be keeping his head, although his life-style did change somewhat. He drove a Rolls now, and had moved to a huge penthouse co-op overlooking Lake Michigan. Ronnie, on the other hand, was enjoying none of the benefits of money and fame. He was still getting by on ten dollars a week—old Mr. Colter wouldn't release a penny out of the trust. "Not until you tell your father," he said. Ronnie was bursting with all his frustrations when he got hit with a *new* decision to make.

"It's time you did a personal, kid." Aben was on the phone.

"A personal appearance? You serious?" Ronnie was in shock.

"Sure, Ron. You can handle it."

"Where?"

"I figured we'd do it at The Auditorium—right here in Chicago. That way you won't be away from home for more than the day."

"What about rehearsals?"

"No sweat. We'll use your record guys. They know the routines, and we'll have the whole place set up and the sound checked before you get there."

Ronnie was quiet.

"What do you say, kid? . . . You there?" Aben was waiting.

"Yeah, I'm here."

"Well . . . ?"

"Still masked?" Ronnie knew what to expect.

"Of course."

Finally Ronnie answered. "Okay, Aben. Go ahead. Can you make it a Saturday?"

"Already had that figured. Will let you know the date. Bye, kid."

"Bye, Aben."

It was done. If Ronnie was nervous, he didn't seem to show it . . . at least not yet. The date was set for a month away. In the meantime, Ronnie was busy working on the songs for his third album, so I didn't see as much of him as usual. We did walk to school every day, and of course saw each other in class, but it wasn't quite the same.

The day of the concert came fast enough. Like Aben had said, seats were gone the first morning they were put on sale—just as much time as it took to process the line, a mile long, waiting at the box office. There were front-page pictures in the newspapers of kids camping out at The Auditorium a full week ahead to get good seats.

Aben brought Ronnie in early that Saturday morning, although the concert wasn't scheduled until 8:00 P.M. The stage door was clear, and Ronnie was hustled into his dressing room, where he could take off his mask and relax until show time. They had his suite fixed nice with a big color TV set, a couch to take a nap if he wanted, magazines to read, and plenty of cold cuts and stuff to eat and drink.

Outside, the security was being set up. The police were everywhere, and Aben had hired his own private forces as well. They even had the riot squad standing by. I understand the cops were very nervous.

Aben gave me two tickets. Big deal! Other than that, I wasn't any part of the whole thing. As I look back, I couldn't have told you where I *should* have been involved. There was no place for me, and just hanging around wouldn't have accomplished anything except run the risk of identifying Ronnie. But just the same, I resented it. There was a knot in my gut, and I had to do something about it. I was going to have a talk with Ronnie.

Anyway, I wasn't about to miss the concert and decided to take Darlene. I picked her up at the apartment, which fortunately was within walking distance to The Auditorium. She kept asking how I had managed to get seats, and I made up a story about a friend of mine who worked in P.R. and had given me two tickets. (At these prices, she should have known better!) The streets were jammed with kids, and four different guys asked if I had tickets to sell. One man with his son offered me two hundred dollars for the pair. Believe me, I was tempted. I sure could have used the money. If Darlene hadn't been with me, I might have done it.

We had to show our tickets to get through the barricades, and finally got inside and found our seats. They were in the top-price section, but in the back part of it, and on the side. That *really* pissed me off. But Darlene thought they were great.

The Auditorium was jammed, mostly with kids. There were cops in all the aisles, and a whole string of them, not more than six feet apart, were lined up in front of the first row. I felt funny. I kept thinking that I was the only person in the whole place who knew that it was just Ronnie Finkelhof who was going to walk out on that stage.

Finally the lights went down, the curtain up, and the concert started with a rock group that Aben had hired to open the show. At that point the kids got more noisy—nobody was paying much attention. They were there only for the main attraction. Then, after about a half hour, the group took their bows to some applause and whistles, along with a few catcalls, and the curtain came down. They were setting up for Spartacus.

When the curtain went up again, all the guys were in place, and a new backdrop had been lowered, showing the famous Spartacus logo. A voice over the loudspeaker system announced, "Ladies and gentlemen, The Auditorium is proud and pleased to present the first personal appearance, anywhere in the world, of the one and only . . . Spartacus!"

Of course, the words were drowned out by screams and yells. Then Ronnie, masked and in his same old blue jeans, western shirt, and hat, walked out on the stage and took his place in front of the microphone. He turned to the group, beat off the tempo, and the first number started. The noise was so deafening that we couldn't hear much, but a lot of people started shushing, and finally the kids quieted down for the last half of the number. That happened on almost every song, and the concert was a blur of noise and excitement. Ronnie was on for about an hour, and after that did three encores. Finally he had to get off, but the screaming wouldn't stop. Sitting on the side as I was, I could see Aben in the wings, sending him out front for a final bow. That's when it happened.

The kids were all on their feet and pushing forward toward the stage. The cops in the back tried to come down to help the ones in front, but they couldn't get through. There was a surge of bodies that began to look dangerous. The steps had been taken away from the sides, and there was an orchestra pit, so it was almost impossible to get at Ronnie, but just the same, it was scary.

Then someone yelled, "Take it off." Pretty soon ev-

eryone picked up the chant. "Take it off, take it off, take
it off . . ." It swelled like a cheer at a football stadium.

Suddenly, out of nowhere, a teenage girl landed on the
side of the stage. She had stood on the railing of the
front box at the side of the auditorium and jumped. The
height must have been fifteen feet at least, and it's a
wonder she didn't break a leg, although we found out
later she had sprained her ankle. Nevertheless, she went
at Ronnie and flung her arms around him in a bear hug
that had him paralyzed. His mask was one that went over
his head, so it couldn't fall off, but she started pulling at
it from the top. Six policemen and Aben came running
out onstage and grabbed her, and it was some funny
sight. They were trying to pull her apart from Ronnie
while the audience was screaming "take it off," and
cheering her on. Cameras were flashing, and the girl
hung tight. Then another kid jumped from the same box,
a boy this time, and others were standing and looking
down to see if they dared jump, too. The boy did hurt
himself, and couldn't get up, and that discouraged the
rest.

Finally the cops half carried both Ronnie and the girl
offstage, and separated them with a little more force than
they were prepared to use in front of what was becoming
an uncontrollable mob. The house lights were up, and
the loudspeaker was blaring that everyone should leave.
Darlene and I ducked out a side exit—it was getting dangerous. We found out in the papers the next day that a
number of kids had been trampled, and two of them hurt
seriously. Pictures were on the front pages again.

I took Darlene to her apartment and caught a late bus
home. The next day was Sunday, and I didn't see or hear
from Ronnie. Somehow I didn't feel like calling him,
and he never called me. But Monday morning, on the

way to school, there was Ronnie Finkelhof waiting for
me as usual. It all seemed weird.

Ronnie was subdued, more like his old self. I think
the experience shook him up, and set him back a peg.
As a result, we fell into our old relationship. I kind of
forgot my peeve, and felt better about things. I guess
what it amounted to was that Ronnie needed me again.
And I knew he *was* my friend.

"Making records is one thing," Ronnie said. "Even
taping a television show isn't so bad. But a personal appearance in front of all those people is something else.
It's getting to me, Sam."

"How did you ever get out of there Saturday night?"
I asked.

"Aben had planned for me to mix with the crowd
again, but we felt with that mob it was too risky. So he
called Brinks armored cars, told them the problem, and
asked if they could help. The police cleared a path to the
stage door, and the armored car backed up against it so
that there was no space in between. Aben and I went in,
they clanged the doors shut, and off we rattled before
anyone could follow. We were dropped off at Aben's car,
which he had parked away from the auditorium, and that
was it."

"What next?" I asked.

"I don't know, Sam." Ronnie seemed upset. "This
isn't like with any other rock star. I know fans sometimes
get out of hand, but last night was something more than
that. I think it's the damn mask. You heard them yell
'take it off!' The kids are beginning to resent it. They're
into my music, sure, but they don't like my hiding from
them."

"But the whole mystery gimmick worked for you."

"At first. But I don't like what happened last night.

Tearing off my mask has become a challenge. I don't dare appear anymore. That mob last night was my fans all right, but they were angry, too. I could feel it.''

"What are you going to do, Ron?" It was good having him confide in me again.

"Damned if I know. But one thing is for sure. Things can't go on this way. I've got to have a talk with Aben."

CHAPTER

25

Aben was out of town that week, so Ronnie had to bide his time. To make matters worse, a complication came up at home. Our semester grades were posted, and Ronnie got his first B. In psychology! Not that that's so terrible, but his father got very high-handed about it. He had already commented about Ronnie being out so often, and getting home late.

"Where were you last Saturday? You were gone all day, and didn't come home until well after we were asleep—God knows at what hour."

"I went to the Spartacus concert, Dad." Ronnie didn't have to lie to his father.

"You *what*?!!"

"I went to the Spartacus concert. I had to get there early, so I could get in ahead of the crowds." He still wasn't lying.

"You know how I feel about that drivel. You know I

refused to let Debbie go, in spite of her begging and crying and carrying on. Why didn't you ask me first? Where did you get the money?''

"A friend took me. It didn't cost me anything.'' Ronnie still wasn't telling his father a lie. "And I think I'm big enough to do things on my own, Dad. I'm not a child. I'm seventeen years old.''

"You may be seventeen years old, but you still don't know what's best for you. If you had stayed home more and paid attention to your studies, you wouldn't have gotten that B.''

"But Dad—''

"Ronnie, being a teenager is one of the most difficult times in life. Don't you think I understand that? So if I seem hard on you, know it's in your own interests.''

"But Dad, that's the only B I've ever had in high school. And it's not a final grade. Everything else has been A's. Besides, it was in psychology, and our teacher is a jerk. He doesn't know beans.''

"Who are you, that you think you know more than your teacher!''

"What does it matter? I'm still first in my class, and I've got my acceptance to Harvard. So what's the big deal?'' It was unusual for Ronnie to argue with his father.

"The big deal is that you've spoiled your record. The big deal is that you've lost your discipline. The big deal, Ronnie, is that from now on you stay home nights, until school is over. That's the big deal!'' Mr. Finkelhof was losing his cool.

"Dad, that's ridiculous. You're treating me like a baby.'' Ronnie, too, was running out of patience with this whole situation.

Mr. Finkelhof wasn't used to back talk. "And since

you want to argue about it, you get no allowance for the next two weeks.''

I guess something snapped in Ronnie at that, and he overreacted. "I don't need your paltry ten dollars, Dad.'' He *still* wasn't lying! "With you, everything is *your* way, the way *you* want it! You have no consideration for what is going on in *my* life. You don't even *know* what I'm into, and I can't tell you because you are too stubborn, won't listen, and wouldn't understand anyway. . . . '' Once Ronnie got started, he couldn't stop.

"Ronnie, I'm warning you—'' Mr. Finkelhof was getting red in the face.

"You want me to be *you*. I'm not. I'm *me*. I've got my own life to lead, and if you had any sensitivity at all to other people, let alone your own son, you'd not only understand that, but you'd encourage it.''

"Ronnie, you stop—'' Mr. Finkelhof was just as surprised at this outburst as he was angry. But Ronnie would *not* stop.

"There's a lot you don't know about me, Dad. Things that would surprise the hell out of you.''

"We can do without the profanity, Ronnie. You know I don't allow those words in this house.''

"Tough.''

"Ronnie!!!!! Go to your room!''

"Sure. But I'm gonna say one more thing. You're my father, and I respect that. But you've got to let up. I can't go on leading a secret life from you. I'd like to talk to you about a lot of things, but you make it impossible.'' There were tears running down Ronnie's face at that point. "Just remember this conversation, and maybe someday, when you get to know what's going on with me, you'll understand.''

Ronnie turned and went to his room. It didn't seem

possible that he could have stood up to the old man like that. But the frustrations of his double life were getting to him, and he damn well couldn't handle it anymore. He plain freaked.

"Imagine *me*, Spartacus, Number-One star in the country, worth maybe seventy-five million dollars, not allowed to go out at night!" he told me. "And my stinking ten-dollar-a-week allowance being cut off!"

It was weird, weird.

A great deal of tension hung over the Finkelhof household for the next week. I'm sure Ronnie's father had some second thoughts about that encounter, but he wasn't the type ever to admit he was wrong. However, a couple of days after the incident, he did make a feeble attempt to find out what was on Ronnie's mind, and what Ronnie meant about "things that would surprise him."

"Ronnie, are you in some kind of trouble? Tell me!" It was said more like an accusation than a concerned expression of interest, even though Mr. Finkelhof didn't mean it the way it sounded. Like a lot of men, he had a problem with showing his feelings, and, of course, Ronnie took it the wrong way.

"No, Dad, I'm not in any trouble."

"Ronnie, now look here—"

"It's *okay*, Dad. I'm fine."

Ronnie would not carry the conversation any further, and Mr. Finkelhof finally backed away. If the old fool had handled himself right, if he had gotten through to Ronnie and shown just an ounce of concern and compassion—which he probably really felt—Ronnie would have poured out his whole painful secret. But Mr. Finkelhof just didn't know how. As I look back, I feel sorry for the man.

Meanwhile, at school, the Spartacus concert was the

big item of discussion. Only a few kids had managed to get in, and they were the center of attention. One of them was Ginny. Her old man had pull in the big city, and had presented his precious daughter with two tickets. She had taken Andy.

"He was fantastic," Ginny said. She was surrounded by a group of kids at recess, and Ronnie had joined them. As I said, he was getting a little bolder, not that anyone paid any attention.

"What does he look like?" someone asked.

"Well, you couldn't see his face," Ginny said. "His whole head was covered. But he's tall, and I could see by the outline of the mask that he's really good-looking."

"I doubt that," Ronnie suddenly piped up.

"What do you know! You weren't even there." She brushed Ronnie off with that curt reply, and proceeded to describe the whole concert, the excitement, the kids on the stage, the pushing and shoving, the police—all of it with great coloring and some exaggeration. Ginny was carried away with the importance of her knowledge, and she went on and on. Ronnie listened for a while, and then left. Nobody noticed.

We spent a lot of time together the remainder of that week, talking things over. Apart from his other problems, Ronnie seemed confused about his feelings for Ginny. I don't think it was the constant rejection, but more a change in Ronnie. Maybe he was seeing her in a different light. But no matter what, she was still some good-looker, and Ronnie was stuck with that.

Finally Aben got back to town, and Ronnie reached him on the phone. "I've got to see you, Aben. Face-to-face. It's important."

"Sure, kid. Tomorrow okay?"

"Yeah, that's fine. Where shall we meet?"

Aben thought for a minute. "We have to be very careful, Ronnie. Tell you what. You know the intersection of Route 137 with the main highway? It's a bus stop."

"Sure. I've passed it often enough."

"Take the Chicago bus and get off there. I'll park my car up 137 a few hundred yards."

After Aben hung up, Ronnie realized he didn't have bus fare, and he wasn't about to ask his dad to reinstate his allowance. So he went to see Mr. Colter.

"I can't do that, Ronnie. You know our understanding. You have signed over total control of the trust to me, and the funds are not to be invaded until you reach your majority."

"But Mr. Colter! I have an important meeting to go to. How do you expect me to handle my affairs?"

"I'm sorry, Ronnie."

"This is ridiculous!"

"The whole thing is ridiculous. But I will not take the responsibility of giving you money without your father's approval. You *could* make life a lot easier for both of us, you know. *Tell* your father. Tell him *now*." Colter was holding that over Ronnie's head.

"Tell my *father*? If he finds out, it won't be from me!"

"What is it, Ronnie? What's the matter?"

"Nothing. Nothing, Mr. Colter. I'm sorry I bothered you."

Ronnie left. Colter wanted to do the right thing, but he had his own problems.

It was a tough week for Ronnie all around.

CHAPTER

26

Ronnie borrowed bus fare from me; he said Aben would pay me back. In fact, Ronnie got into a whole thing about how he was going to ask Aben to give me a job at the studio on his recording dates. He even said Aben could take the money out of royalties going to his trust as a cost of the session.

"You do a lot for me, Sam," he said. "You should get *something* out of all this."

"No deal, Ron. It would be charity. Besides, I don't want to be *working* for you. You and I are friends, and that's how I want it to stay."

"It'll always be like that, Sam. But there's no reason you can't take—"

"Forget it, Ron. Pass. I appreciate what you're trying to do, but I would rather leave things the way they are. Really."

Ronnie gave me a long look, and then smiled. "Okay, buddy. But somewhere down the road I'll be in a position to do something for you. And whatever you want, you'll have it. Even if it's only free legal advice." Ronnie laughed.

"That I'll probably need," I said, smiling back. I was grateful to Ronnie for making the offer, but I couldn't see myself taking a handout, even though he could well afford it.

That afternoon we caught the bus for Chicago, and got off where Aben had told us. His Rolls was parked nearby, and we headed on up the road. Aben swung the doors open as we approached, Ronnie got in the front seat, and I climbed in the back.

"Hi, fellas. How we doin'?" Aben was in his usual good mood.

"Not very well, Aben."

"What's the matter, Ronnie?"

"We've got to make some kind of move. I'm not prepared to go on like this." Ronnie was very serious.

"Hey, listen, kid, do you know how much we raked in last week? Your share alone was—"

"Aben, listen. I don't care how much it was. We both have enough for the rest of our lives."

"Then what is it?" Aben looked nervous.

"You once said we would come out of hiding when this whole mystery man thing reached its peak. Well, I think we're a little past that already."

"How can you say that? We could have sold ten times as many tickets to that concert. Do you know the film and TV offers that are on my desk? This thing is just beginning to—"

"Aben, please. It's not box office I'm talking about. It's something else. My fans are beginning to resent my mask. There was anger mixed in with love at that concert last week. Couldn't you feel it?"

"That was only your first personal appearance. How can you come up with an idea like that? Were you afraid of the mob, is that it? You know you'll be protected. We'll have twice as much security next time if you want. We'll—"

"There'll be no next time, Aben." Ronnie said it in a very slow, deliberate way.

Aben looked at him for a minute. He could see that Ronnie was totally serious. Aben was finally facing up to the fact that he, Aben, wasn't Spartacus—Ronnie was. Aben was dealing with a human being, one with emotions and a mind of his own. Spartacus was no longer a faceless entity that he could steer and direct any way he pleased. Aben argued a bit longer, but feebly. When he knew that was it, he gave in and laid it in Ronnie's lap.

"Okay, kid, if you feel that strongly. I thought we had it made for quite a while longer. But now that you bring it up, I have to admit that I've been feeling a backlash, too. The jockeys aren't playing the game anymore. They spin your records because they have to, but I also feel a resentment. And if you won't do personals, we've got to change our act."

I think Aben had recognized the problem just as much as Ronnie, but by my way of thinking, he just didn't want to give up his role, and have the *real* Spartacus stand up. Now maybe he had no choice.

"All right, Ronnie," Aben went on. "You name it. What do we do now?"

"I've been thinking about it a lot, Aben, and it's got to be one of three things. First, I'm willing to go on making records, and nothing else. No TV, no film, and no personals."

"That's out, Ronnie. We'd be dead in a year. An act has to be seen to sustain record success. No matter how good your stuff is from here on, you'd soon lose your fans."

"I understand. Okay, second choice is to quit altogether. No more records, no nothing. No one will ever know who Spartacus is, and it will all soon be history. I'm prepared for that, too.''

"That's worse than the first idea, Ronnie! How can you think of throwing the whole thing in the toilet? Besides, you can't give up writing and performing. It's got to be in your blood by now." Aben looked really upset. That would blow his whole way of life. "Give me the third idea before I have a heart attack!"

"The third idea is the obvious one, but now that the time has come, I don't know if I'm prepared to go through with it."

"You mean come out?" Aben jumped in.

"Right. But you know what that means. My whole life would be over. I mean, this part of it. I graduate high school next week. I'm supposed to enter Harvard in the fall. How can I do any of that?"

"But I thought you *wanted* to come out. You brought it up a long time ago. You said you felt ready."

"I thought I did, Aben. But suddenly now I'm not so sure. You saw what happened at that concert."

"The concert. *That's* what blew your mind." Ronnie didn't answer. "Wasn't it?" Aben was beginning to get the message.

"Let's just say it woke me up to reality, what's happened to me—and what my life would be like." Ronnie was not being emotional, just very somber and serious.

Aben was quiet for a long time. So was Ronnie. I just sat there in the backseat of the Rolls listening. I felt I should stay out of it. It was something Ronnie had to figure out for himself. Finally Aben broke the silence.

"Okay, Ronnie. I dig it. You know, kid, you're the first artist I've ever had that I feel about the way I do. You're a fantastic young man, and I don't mind telling you I've come to love you like a son. Business is business, but I'm not going to screw up your life, or even try to help you do it to yourself. I'll go along with whatever you want to do. We'll just make records, or we'll quit altogether if that's what you want, and my lips will be sealed forever. Or if you decide to come out and do the whole bit, you know I'll be there to help you in every way I can."

"Gee, Aben, I—"

"Don't say another word, Ronnie. Go home and think about it. Sleep on it. Take all the time you want. I'll handle things in the meantime, and when you're ready, call me. I'll be there."

Ronnie tried to thank Aben, but he just shushed him up, told us to get on home, and then waited until we were safely on the bus before he drove off. Aben had surprised both of us. It was the first time we had seen that side of him.

Maybe Aben was a softy after all; maybe it *wasn't* all dollars and cents with him. Of course, by now he had enough loot and could *afford* to be generous. Or maybe he was just playing it cool with Ronnie, and sucking him in. In any event, at the time we both accepted Aben at face value.

But Mr. Nice Guy Sam got screwed as usual. We had forgotten to ask Aben to pay me back for bus fare.

CHAPTER

27

The decisions most teenage boys wrestle with have to do with girls—what high school courses to take—girls—what colleges to apply to—girls—and like that. But Ronnie had to face up to a *major* choice. And the lines were clearly drawn in his head. He had had enough exposure to the problems of being a superstar not to be taken in by only the glamour and excitement. And acceptance at Harvard was a rare privilege that he fully appreciated. These were truly serious way-of-life alternatives. And neither of them involved a question of speculation; they were both already there for him, just for the taking. Furthermore, the time for decision was now.

Ronnie struggled with the problem. It was never out of his head. It wasn't that he talked about it so much—it was just that he was totally preoccupied. Sometimes he didn't even answer when I spoke to him.

That was some dilemma. On the one hand, there was fame, money, travel, the high life, and anything material he wanted, but it was coupled with a total loss of privacy, the problems of security, the press looking over his shoulder with every move, the demands on his time, the responsibilities. Ronnie somewhere understood it all. On the other hand, there was the prestige of Harvard, a great education, normal life-style, and then, of course, pleasing his father. In spite of everything, that was still on his mind.

On top of all that, Debbie was getting worrisome. She threatened to talk if she didn't get her diary back. "Go ahead and read it," she said. "I don't care anymore!" The truth is that she was so caught up in the excitement of Spartacus that she just couldn't contain such a delicious secret much longer. Ronnie finally pinned her down in her room one afternoon.

"Debbie, I've got to talk to you," he said.

"So talk." Debbie didn't make it easy.

"If you tell one person who I am—just one—it will be all over the country within days. There's no way even your best friend could keep it to herself. It's news—big news. It's even worth a lot of money to an informer. And you are the one I must look to for protection."

"What's so terrible if it did get out?"

"Debbie, what do you think it would do to our home? Think of Dad—Mom—all of us. Our lives would never be the same. Who's your favorite record star? Michael Jackson? Bruce Springsteen? Imagine one of them living in our house as part of our family. Don't you understand? It would be the end of our lives—at least the way it's been."

Debbie was thoughtful; she was beginning to get the picture. "Well what are you going to do?"

"I don't know, kid sister. If I want to go to Harvard in the fall, and on to law school, I've got to *kill* Spartacus—and I've got to do it now."

"Is that what you want?"

"I wish I knew . . . I wish I knew. I've got to think some more. But give me time—a little more time. Please." Ronnie was in a state, and Debbie saw it. It upset her. She had the problem laid right in her lap, and was part of it whether she liked it or not.

"I'm sorry, Ronnie. I guess I didn't understand. I didn't think. I'm sorry. I really am. I . . . I won't say a word. I promise. I absolutely really *promise*." Debbie was pretty emotional herself by that time.

"Thanks, Debbie."

"Ronnie?"

"Yes?"

"Can I have my diary back now?"

Ronnie looked at her. "Is it *that* important to you?"

"Please, Ronnie."

"Okay, sure. I trust you. It's in my closet on the top shelf, behind the encyclopedias."

Debbie retrieved her precious book of secrets and was glad to get out of there. She was afraid she might start to bawl, although she really didn't understand why. That same afternoon Ronnie called and asked me to come over. He seemed satisfied that Debbie would be okay, but the big problem on his mind was still unresolved. A decision had to be made, and soon.

"What do I do, Sam?" Ronnie said.

"I refuse to answer on the grounds that it might incriminate me." I wasn't about to influence him.

"Really, Sam. I've got to talk to someone. It can't be my father, and even if Aben would take a stand, I'd have to consider he was looking out for himself."

"What about Colter? Do you think it would be any help to talk to him?"

"I don't think so. But I've got to talk to somebody. What can I lose?"

But Mr. Colter wouldn't commit himself. "That's a decision only you can make, Ronnie," he said. "And if you want help or advice, go to your father. I can't take

the responsibility of advising you one way or the other.''
I guess you couldn't blame the old guy.

Another week, and Ronnie was becoming a basket
case. Finally, on Saturday morning, he called.

"Can you come over, Sam?"

"Sure. What's up?"

"I want to talk to you before I call Aben. . . . I've
made a decision!"

CHAPTER

28

Mrs. Finkelhof answered the door.
"Hello, Sam. Ronnie is in his room."

"Hi, Mrs. Finkelhof."

"Sam, could I talk to you for a minute?"

"Sure, Mrs. Finkelhof."

"It's about Ronnie. I'm worried about him. He seems
so . . . well, so preoccupied, so distant. And he doesn't
look well. You're his best friend, and I thought maybe
you'd know if there's something wrong. Everytime I ask
him he just says, 'Nothing, Mom. I'm fine.' "

"Golly, Mrs. Finkelhof, I . . . I don't know. There's
nothing wrong that I know of." All I wanted to do was
get away from her and up to Ronnie's room.

"Are you sure he's not in some kind of trouble? You
can tell me."

"I'm sure he's not in any trouble, Ma'am." I guess that was no lie.

"Well, Sam, please, if you learn of anything you think his father and I should know, will you tell us? It would be in his own interests."

"Sure, Mrs. Finkelhof. I sure will." That gave me my out, and I hurried upstairs. Ronnie was staring out the window when I got to his room, kind of in a daze. But he quickly came to life.

"Sit down, Sam," he said. I sat, but Ronnie kept pacing the whole time he talked.

"I'm going to do it. I'm going to be Spartacus." He looked at me and waited just a second for a reaction. I didn't know what I should say, but he hardly gave me an opening, and quickly went on, very animated. "I've thought and thought and thought about it, and there's no other way. No going back now. How can I give up my music?" Again he didn't wait for an answer. "I've learned what it is to have other people like my songs. And me. Love *me*, Sam!"

"I know what you're saying, Ron. I understand." I felt I had to say *something*, although the truth is I was taking all this with mixed emotions.

But Ronnie didn't seem to hear me. He rattled on. About his music, and how people related to it—and how he had *more* to say in his lyrics. What reviewers wrote about him: his poetry, and his talent. Praise and recognition can be a heady experience, but to someone like Ronnie the effect was doubly exhilarating. I let him go on. The best thing I could do at that point was to just listen.

Finally Ronnie paused, and said, "What do you think?"

I guess I knew the answer to what I was about to ask, but I had to bring it up. "What about your education?"

"I'm not going to Harvard. It can't be done half-way. Got to be one or the other, and it's gonna be Spartacus—all the way!"

"Is it worth it, Ron?"

"Worth it? Sam, do you *really* know what my life has been like? Do you understand what it is to be the ugly duckling? The class goon? Kids call me Finkelschmuck behind my back. 'There goes Finkelschmuck,' they say. I never told *anyone* I've heard them—not even you."

"Ron, has it been *that* bad?"

"That bad, Sam. You and I have been very close, and you know me better than anyone in this world. But you can't *feel* for me. At least in *my* head, that's the way it's been."

"But things would change. I'm sure they would as you got older."

"Maybe. But all I know is that I have visions of never getting married, living alone all my life, going to an office every day to sit in a two-by-four cubicle writing contracts or reading case histories. And maybe being under my father's thumb even at work. I have nightmares about it."

I guess I never realized the depth of Ronnie's feelings. "But is *Spartacus* the answer?" I said. "Are you *sure* it's the right move?"

"Sam, being Spartacus has done something for me that twenty years on a psychiatrist's couch couldn't do. I'm learning to appreciate myself—to *like* myself. I've got talent. I write great songs. I sing. People love me. I never experienced the feeling before. Even though it's not Ronnie Finkelhof they see, I still get an idea of what it's like."

"What about the problems—the concerts, no privacy—all that?"

"I'll make it very simple for you. Suppose one day a fairy princess appeared and said, 'Sam Bennett, all you have to do is say the word *alakazam*, and you will turn white.' What would you do?"

I couldn't answer. At first I thought I knew what I would do. Why not . . . who was I kidding? Then I decided I shouldn't deny my race. But was that a good reason, or just a cop-out? A great deal flashed through my mind in that brief minute. No one had ever asked me such a question before, and I was annoyed at Ronnie for putting me on the spot. Whitey figures we all want to be them, was all I could think. But then I knew that's not the way it is. We have to be who we are—and I have to be me. Black is who I am, and black is who I stay. I'd miss my color, strange as it may sound—and I wasn't about to lose my soul.

"Sorry, Sam." Ronnie spoke before I could figure out how to get my feelings through to him. I must have been staring into space. "I guess that's not a very fair question. I was only trying to make a comparison."

"Let's just say you made your point," I said. There was an awkward pause, and I changed the subject. "How you gonna handle your family . . . your father?"

"I've thought and thought about that. But I have to *stop* thinking. My dad brought all this on himself. It didn't have to be this way. He could have been part of it. Anyway, look at the money I'll have, and the things I can do for them. And I will, too. That should make up for a lot."

Ronnie had stopped pacing and was standing there looking at me. I knew what he was after. So I did it. I stood up, clapped him on the back, and said, "You're doing the right thing, buddy. Absolutely no question. I would do the same. It's the only way. Go for it, man.''

"Thanks, Sam. I knew you'd understand.'' Tears puddled up in Ronnie's eyes as he stood looking at me, even though he was smiling. Then he gave me a big hug. I had never known him to be so demonstrative, and was a little embarrassed, but also pleased.

"And Sam, you're gonna be with me. All the way. We'll work that out, too.'' The last part I hadn't expected, and it gave *me* something to think about.

We called Aben that same day and gave him the news. Aben didn't react either positively or negatively. He just said, "You sure, Ronnie? Absolutely sure?'' When Ronnie had convinced him that it was final, Aben said, "Okay, kid. Sit tight. I'll figure out how to handle it, and give you a call. In the meantime, do nothing. This has to be orchestrated just right. You relax and take it easy.''

School was over, and Ronnie and I just hung out together. Now that the decision was behind us, we talked a lot about what it was going to be like from here on. Even though Ronnie's position was firm, he still spent a great deal of time justifying it.

"I'll do it differently, Sam.'' We were sitting in his room. "I'll find a way to make my life normal, or at least close to normal. I'll never get into drugs or anything like that.''

"I'm sure you won't, Ronnie.'' That's one thing that wouldn't have entered my head.

"I'll get a retreat someplace where I can get away from everything when I want to. And I don't have to work and be in the limelight *all* the time. I can take off *half* the time—six months a year if I want.''

"Sure, Ronnie.''

"Nobody can make me do anything or be anywhere I don't want to be. I'm boss of my own life. Nobody will own me."

"Of course."

"I'll do it differently. You'll see."

"I'm sure you will, Ron." I was beginning to feel that he was trying to talk himself into something, and the more he went on, the more I wondered if he really *could* do it differently.

We were quiet for a while. Then I asked Ronnie the question that he still hadn't answered. "How you gonna handle your old man?"

Ronnie didn't reply. He was looking out the window.

"Ronnie . . . ?" He just kept staring.

"He's got to find out sooner or later," I said.

Finally Ronnie turned and looked at me. "I know, Sam. I've thought about it a lot. How . . . when . . . all that."

"And . . . ?"

"I'm not going to tell him now."

"You're not?"

"No, Sam." Ronnie continued looking at me for a minute. Then he turned away, and very quietly said, "He's going to find out the hard way."

CHAPTER

27 It was almost three weeks later that Aben finally called. We were both at Ronnie's house.

"I've got it all planned," he told Ronnie. "We've got to have a meetin'."

"Same place?" Ronnie asked.

"No, let's do it at my office on Saturday. It will be closed, and I don't see any problem. That way we can spend some time and talk this all out."

"Fine," Ronnie said. "Two o'clock okay?"

"Perfect."

"Sam's here. I'll bring him along."

"By all means."

When Ronnie hung up, he looked at me with a funny kind of anxious grin. "Well, here we go, buddy," he said.

"Yeah," I said, "here we go."

On Saturday, Ronnie and I caught the bus and arrived at the Jetstream building a few minutes early. We rang the night bell, and Aben was right there to let us in. The place was empty, and seemed very quiet and kind of spooky as we walked back to Aben's office. It was just as cluttered as ever, except that the phones weren't ringing all the time.

"Sit down, boys. We've got a lot to talk about." Aben

looked more serious than usual, and wasted no time getting to the point. "We're going to have a Spartacus concert at the biggest arena we can find," he said. "We'll
announce that Spartacus will take off his mask—that he
has decided to come out and identify himself. I've already retained Rogers and Cowan, one of the best public
relations firms in the entertainment business, with offices
in both Beverly Hills and New York. They'll get us tremendous press. This concert will be the biggest thing the
industry has ever seen. I'm thinking of doing it in New
York, at Madison Square Garden." Aben was getting
excited just talking about it, and rattled on with his plans
while Ronnie and I sat listening quietly.

Finally Ronnie interrupted. "Wait, Aben. Please."

"What is it, Ronnie?"

"I don't want to do it in New York."

"Why? We'll get the best coverage there, and Madison Square Garden holds more than any—"

"I know, Aben. But I want it to be in Chicago, or at
least in the Chicago area."

"Why, Ronnie? If you're coming out, you don't have
logistic problems. You can go anywhere—"

"I know, but I have my reasons."

Aben looked at me. I knew the answer, but didn't
think I should speak for Ronnie. There was a long pause,
so I finally broke the silence. "Do it his way, Aben," I
said. "There are a few people here that I'm sure Ronnie
wants to be at the concert." I was thinking of Ginny in
particular.

Aben got the message. "Okay, Ronnie," he said. "I
guess after all you've been through, you should have that
choice. I'll go along."

"I don't mean to create a problem . . ."

"No problem, Ronnie. Don't worry about it. Only thing is where to do it."

"How about The Auditorium, where we were last time?"

"Too small. We could go into the Airie Crown—holds maybe four to five thousand. But even that's too small."

"How many people do you think will come?" Ronnie asked.

Aben laughed. "As many as we have room for, kid, as many as we have room for. The best bet may be to go outdoors. I'm thinking of Soldier Field."

"That's a football stadium," Ronnie said.

"Sure, but they have big events there. I think maybe that's it. I'll make a call first thing Monday and see if we can get a date."

"You sure, Aben? A *football* stadium? That place must hold a hundred thousand people."

"So? Not to worry. Leave everything to me. I haven't let you down yet, have I?"

Ronnie didn't answer at first. The thought of appearing in Soldier Field was not quite what he had in mind, but finally he agreed. "Okay, Aben, whatever you say . . . if you think you can handle that big a deal."

"No sweat, kid. Now we've got to set the date. How soon are you ready for this?"

"I'm ready now, so the sooner the better." Then Ronnie laughed. "Before I change my mind!"

"Ronnie, once you turn me loose, there'll be no change of mind, no turning back."

"I know, Aben. I was only kidding. Don't worry, I'll be there when the time comes."

"Okay, Ronnie. I start to work next week. One more thing. The Grammy Awards are coming up, and you've got a lot of nominations."

"How does all that work?"

"It's the National Association of Recording Arts and Sciences. We call it NARAS. People from the whole record industry—artists, songwriters, executives—I'm a member, of course. It's like the Oscars. We vote to pick the winners in various categories, and then there's the big awards ceremony, and the television show."

"I know. I've seen it. What if I win something?"

"I don't think there's much 'what if' about it. But I don't want you there. You'd have to go to Los Angeles. It's too risky, and with your coming-out concert so close, why take any chances?"

"What do we do?"

"Nothing. I'll be in L.A. and will accept for you. That okay?"

"Sure. That's fine," Ronnie said. But he had a touch of disappointment in his voice.

"Well, guys. I guess that about does it," Aben said. We talked for a while longer, just reminiscing over all that had happened, and what was about to happen. It was getting exciting, and my pulse was up a few beats just thinking about the concert.

Yet at the same time, I had an uneasy feeling.

CHAPTER

30⭐

Aben called the following Tuesday. "I've got August twelfth," he said. "It's the first Saturday the stadium is free, and any later gets into football season. I have it for the whole day so we can set up, and I'm scheduling the concert for 8:00 P.M."

"That sounds fine, Aben," Ronnie said. The twelfth was only five weeks away.

"This is probably the most important appearance you'll ever make, Ronnie," Aben said. "We have to plan it very carefully. I want to talk to you about what numbers you'll do, how we get you there, what you'll wear . . ."

Ronnie didn't argue with any of Aben's thoughts, except for one thing. Aben had an idea about dressing him up in some kind of costume, which he wasn't too clear about. But Ronnie put his foot down. "I'm coming into that arena just like before," he said. "My blue jeans, western shirt, and, of course, my mask." He was insistent, so Aben backed down. We weren't sure just what Aben had in mind anyway.

That was the beginning of a very long five weeks for Ronnie. In the meantime the Grammy Awards were held in Hollywood, and we watched it on television. The show had a lot of production numbers, and didn't cover all the awards—only the big ones. Spartacus won for "Best New Artist of the Year." Then he won for the "Best Song of the Year." Then he won for "Best Single Record." Then he won for "Best Album." Then they gave him an "Outstanding Artist" special award. Aben was up onstage accepting every couple of minutes. The emcee said it was the first time any one person had won in all those categories.

Aben knew Spartacus was going to get the special award, so he saved a speech until the last. After he accepted the final Grammy, Aben turned toward the audience. He was wearing a tuxedo, although I had never seen one like it. It was blue, with binding around the lapels. And the shirt had huge ruffles that were edged with blue, and big round studs up the front—there were maybe seven or eight of them. Even his tie was weird; it looked more like a sash than a bow. I guess that's music biz dress. When the applause died down, Aben made his speech.

> Ladies and gentlemen, I am very pleased to accept this, and all the other Grammy Awards, on behalf of Spartacus. He would like to have been here, but for many reasons, that was not feasible. He did tell me, in case he won, that he wanted to thank all of the members of NARAS that have given him this gratifying acclaim, and that he is very proud to be part of the recording industry. Spartacus is many miles from here at this moment, but I know he is watching. I want to thank him, not merely for his contribution to Jetstream Records, but also on behalf of the record manufacturers, distributors, rack jobbers, and retailers who have benefited by what he has done for all of us. Not only has Spartacus been a tremendous stimulation to our business, but he has made an artistic

contribution to the music of America that will live for
many years to come.

I know that there has been a great deal of speculation as to the reasons behind the Spartacus mask. I
want to take this opportunity to tell you that *never*
was this meant to be any kind of publicity stunt. It
was Spartacus's honest and sincere wish—in fact in-
sistence—that his identity not be made known. Of
course, none of us knew in the beginning that he
would be so phenomenally successful. That, of
course, has made maintaining secrecy most difficult.
But now I have been authorized to tell you that Spartacus has decided that it is not possible for him to
continue any longer in this manner, and that he has
come to what, for him, was a most difficult decision.
Ladies and gentlemen, I am pleased to announce that,
on August twelfth, at a concert at Soldier Field in
Chicago, Spartacus will take off his mask, and identify himself to the world!

On his behalf, I thank you again for these most
appreciated awards.

We could hear the audience gasp, and then applaud
loudly. Ronnie and I looked at each other. Aben had not
told us he was going to make the announcement on the
show, but we should have known. In one free minute he
had reached millions of people. It was the kind of commercial that money couldn't buy. He must have planned
it like that from the beginning.

But that was only the opening gun. The story was
picked up by all the wire services the next day. TV news
ran clips of the show with Aben's speech, and later, the
weekly magazines carried pictures of Spartacus taken at
his first concert.

Aben was criticized by NARAS for using the show for
what they called a commercial plug, but he insisted it

was news, not an advertisement. Anyway, the deed was done, and nobody could take it back.

All three TV networks called the next morning wanting to televise the big event, and Aben played one against the other. He finally settled on ABC, and he and Colter worked out the details of the deal.

Now Ronnie had to make his own special plans. First thing he did was to arrange for Aben to see that a block of seats was set aside for Mapleton High School. Mapleton was not singled out—seats were also provided for various other schools in the Chicago area. This was done as a gesture, and publicized as a device to avoid scalpers, as well as unnecessary long lines of teenagers camping out at the box office. What nobody knew was that Mapleton High got the most and best seats in the stadium.

Debbie got four of those seats. The next problem was how to get her father and mother to take her.

"Why don't you tell Mom and Dad who you are and get it over with?" Debbie asked.

"No, Debbie, I want Dad to find out along with everyone else. And I want him to *pay* for the tickets."

"Ronnie, how can I possibly get him to go? Even if the tickets were free, he wouldn't do it!"

"Debbie, if you are ever going to do something for me, this is the time. Please don't ask me why. This is the way I want it, the way I've imagined it. I don't care how—I don't care *what* you do, but get him there. Please."

Well, Debbie rose to the occasion, as only a female can. The next week at the Finkelhof household was one of crying, screaming, and general hysterics. Ronnie told me Debbie was wonderful. She refused to eat. She pretended to be sick. She went into periods of sulking where she wouldn't talk or respond to anyone. A professional actress couldn't have done better.

Finally Mrs. Finkelhof took over. "Ben," she said, "I won't have any more of this. I'm taking Debbie, and Ronnie, too, whether you come or not. Your stubbornness has gone too far, even for me."

I guess Mr. Finkelhof couldn't handle *both* females. Maybe he was also beginning to feel guilty, especially since he and Ronnie had had that argument. So he broke down, and at dinner that night announced that he was taking the whole family to the Spartacus concert.

"Not me, Dad," Ronnie said.

"What do you mean? I thought you'd be delighted. Are you trying to get back at me or something?"

"No, Dad, honest. It's just that I had some plans. And, well, I've been to a Spartacus concert. Once is enough. Take Debbie and Mom. I think that's great."

"Well, I'm glad you feel that way, Ronnie—about Spartacus, I mean. But what about the extra ticket we have? No point in wasting it."

"Why don't you ask Dan Colter, dear?" said Mrs. Finkelhof. "After all, he's alone, and he does represent Spartacus in the firm. He should be there, and I'm sure that he wouldn't want to go by himself."

"Good idea," said Mr. Finkelhof. "I'll call him first thing in the morning. Then when that kid takes off his silly mask, Dan can tell us who he is, where he came from, how he got to our firm, and what all this nonsense is about!"

CHAPTER

31

There's one thing that happened before the big concert I should tell you about, since I have a feeling it was an important event in Ronnie's life—although at the time I couldn't know for sure.

We were having a pizza and talking about nothing but August twelfth, when out of the blue Ronnie said, "Sam, do you mind if I go into town and see Marsha . . . alone?" I was surprised. We had double dated twice after that first visit, both times going to rock concerts in Chicago, but Ronnie still hadn't been totally at ease. He and Marsha talked about music a lot, but he never made any kind of move. And Marsha just played it cool. I think she liked Ronnie, but she for sure could see how shy he was, and probably didn't want to push it. Now he wanted to see her alone!

"Why not," I said, "good idea. You don't have to ask me if you can make a date, for Christ's sake! What's on your mind? As if I didn't know."

"It isn't that. I just want to see if I can handle it. You know . . . on my own."

"Sure, man. Go for it!"

My buddy never did tell me what happened that night. I didn't know if he was being a "gentleman" about it, whether the whole thing was a flop, or what the hell happened. "Hey Ron, open up," I said. But he just smiled, shook his head, and changed the subject. So I called Darlene. You know how girls talk to each other, and I figured *she'd* tell. But all I got was, "Mind your own business, Sam."

I finally gave up.

CHAPTER

32

That last week before the concert was tough for Ronnie. Facing up to unmasking in front of a hundred thousand people and a television audience—and his father—brought out all his old insecurities. He had certainly been improving in past months, but now he seemed to be slipping back into his old ways. As the day of the concert approached, Ronnie was not in the best of shape. For reasons of my own, neither was I.

On D-Day minus one, I decided to go over to Ronnie's house. I was going to get straightened out with him where *I* would be in all this. Aben—big-hearted Aben—had given me *four* tickets to the concert instead of the usual two. Big deal. I had asked Darlene and Marsha, and told Marsha she could bring a date. She suggested Ronnie, but I said I had already asked him, and that he said he hated Spartacus and wouldn't be caught dead at one of his concerts! (Might as well have a little fun.) Marsha was disappointed; she had a warm spot for Ronnie now.

But she was still delighted with the invitation. You'll be more than delighted, I thought.

Ronnie was going over one of his new numbers when I got to his place. "Wow, Sam," he said. "I'm glad you came by."

"What's the problem?" He looked upset.

"I'm scared, buddy. I'm freaked, if you want to know the truth."

Ronnie was looking to me for support, and here I was about to complain about being shunted off every time he made an appearance. "Can I help?" I said.

"Just stick close. I want you backstage with me this time."

"You sure it's okay, Ron? You know how Aben's been about my being around you when you're masked."

"Forget Aben. Nobody we know will see us. Anyway, what's the difference? It will all be over after tomorrow."

I felt ashamed about my own petty problems. I also felt good. Ron was okay, he really was. "I'll be there," I said. "From tomorrow morning, right through the concert. Now for Christ's sake relax. You're gonna be a smash. And wait until Mapleton High gets a load of who their hero is!"

"And you-know-who gets a look at his nonhero." Ronnie managed to laugh. "Thanks, Sam. You always make me feel better."

That night I called Darlene, made some dumb excuse about not being able to pick her up, and said I'd leave the tickets at the box office and meet her there. She could go with Marsha and her date. Then on Saturday I left early with Ronnie for Chicago. He had told his folks he was going to spend the day at the lake, and he would see them when they got back from the concert that night.

Nobody thought anything of it. Then Ronnie picked me up and we took off.

In Chicago, Aben had that same house lined up, and was waiting for us when we arrived shortly before noon.

"We hang out here for just a couple of hours, guys," he said. "I don't want to cut things too close. We're using the Brinks truck to get us in."

"Sam's coming backstage with me, Aben."

"No sweat. It'll work out fine. Brinks is due here at two. Audio is all tested, the band's been going over everything again just to make sure, the light cues are set—everything should go smoothly. I even have—"

Suddenly and unexpectedly Ronnie blurted out, "I'm nervous, Aben. I'm really very uptight." He had apparently been working himself into a state without our realizing it, and he turned pale as a marshmallow in a snowstorm! I must admit I panicked, but Aben stayed quite calm.

"Ronnie . . . come on, kid. You've done this before." Aben spoke very quietly.

"But a hundred thousand people? And television at the same time? Live!"

"Don't think about how many people will be watching," Aben said. "Just do your thing like always. A hundred or a hundred million—what's the difference, Ronnie? The performance is just the same."

"I guess that's not really it. It's . . . it's the mask . . . taking it off. I don't know—I just don't know how I will. . . . Oh God, I think I'm going to be sick."

Ronnie ran for the bathroom, with Aben and me right behind. He made it just in time. When he finally stopped heaving, Aben took his arm and led him into the bedroom. "Lie down here. Just relax, Ronnie. You're going to be all right. I promise you, you're going to be fine."

"I'm sorry," Ronnie said. "I don't know what's the matter with me."

"Don't be sorry, kid," Aben said. "It happens all the time." I was scared for Ronnie, but Aben seemed to be taking it in stride. "Do you know that some of the most seasoned performers in the business toss their cookies before every appearance?" Aben continued. "I've seen the best of them go bonkers just before going on, and then they go out and give the best performance of their lives."

"Really?" Ronnie asked.

"Really," Aben answered. "Now just lie there and take it easy. You're gonna be okay." Aben gave me a nod, and we went back into the living room.

"Don't worry, Sam," he said. "He really *will* be okay."

"You sure, Aben?" I was worried.

"I'm sure. Now let's have some lunch." Aben had a table laid out with cold cuts and beer.

We were just finishing our first sandwich when Ronnie suddenly appeared in the doorway. The color was back in his face, and although he still seemed a little shaky, he looked much better.

"Could I have some lunch, too, you guys? I'm hungry."

"That's the best news I've heard all day," Aben said, and the three of us had a good laugh. Ronnie sat down, Aben opened up another beer, and I made a sandwich for Ronnie and a second one for myself. The food tasted much better after that.

Brinks arrived promptly at 2:00 P.M. Ronnie masked up, and we climbed in the back of the truck. It was like being inside a tin can. We sat on benches along the sides, and rattled along without being able to see outside. It

was a long trip, or at least seemed that way. Finally the
truck drove into the stadium and let us out right on the
edge of the football field. That was kind of a kick, being
there. I had an impulse to race for the goal posts. Too
bad we didn't have a football.

Workmen were still putting last-minute touches on a
platform in the center of the field. Both Ronnie and I
wanted to watch, but Aben hustled us backstage. I think
he didn't want Ronnie to see the setup and get nervous
all over again. We went to the stadium's dressing rooms,
and there was a private office where Ronnie could shut
the door and take off his mask. It had a cot, a table, a
desk, and a couple of chairs, and that's about it—not the
most cozy place to relax, and we had a lot of time until
the concert.

"Had to get you here early," Aben said. "We couldn't
see coming in, but the driver told me there's a mob outside already. The police are having a hard time."

"What do we do now?" Ronnie asked.

"I'm gonna run Sam's extra tickets up to the box office. You just take it easy. Take a nap if you can."

"Oh, sure!" Ronnie said, and we laughed. He seemed
to be in pretty good spirits, but his insides were still in
turmoil.

An hour before concert time the stadium doors were
opened. It was still fairly light out, and I snuck through
the passageway to the field for just a minute to take a
peek. Kids were rushing in the entrances from all sides,
scrambling for their seats in the general admission section. Those in the front with reserved seats were moving a little more slowly, but even they were anxious to
claim their prize locations. The stadium was filled in
what probably was record time. I hoped Darlene and
Marsha would have no trouble holding my place. The

plan was for me to stay with Ronnie until he went on, and then join them. I wanted to see the whole thing from the audience, and then get back and be with him afterward.

I stuck close to Ronnie the rest of the day. Then, about ten after eight, the opening act started. They were a pretty good rock group, and I went back through the tunnel to watch. The field lights were on, but the seating area was dark, except for the reflection of the lights on the first rows, so I couldn't see faces too well. The TV cameras were up in the booth at the top of the stadium like at the games, but there were a lot of still cameramen squatting down on the field. Cops were everywhere. They circled the whole place, even though it would not have been easy to get down from the bleachers.

The opening act was hard rock, and nobody was paying too much attention, at least judging by the noise from the audience. They were scheduled to be on for half an hour. I watched for about ten minutes.

"Where the hell you been, Sam?" Ronnie was upset when I got back. "Jesus, I go on soon."

"Sorry, Ronnie. I just took a look outside. You all right?"

"I guess so. Long as I have the mask on."

"So not to worry," Aben said. "It stays on until the end of the concert, like we planned."

"Yeah. But then it comes off. Oh shit, guys, what am I doing? My father . . . my mother out there . . . kids at school. What am I doing? I shouldn't have gone this far. I shouldn't have done it this way. I must be crazy!" Ronnie was suddenly in a panic again.

"Ronnie!" Aben almost screamed at him. "Knock it off. It's done, and a year from now you'll look back at tonight and laugh. So will your parents. Now settle down.

All you have to think about at the moment is to give the best goddamned performance of your life!''

Ronnie was quiet after that, but he grabbed my hand and hung on, right through the intermission. When we walked out to the edge of the tunnel together, Ronnie was still holding on to me.

The field was totally dark now, except for a number of very bright spotlights beaming directly on the platform in the center of the field. Ronnie's group was already set up, and on an elevated section in front of them was a stool with Ronnie's guitar, and in front of that his microphone. Funny thing—the stadium was strangely quiet. There was kind of an eerie feeling about the whole place.

Ronnie had on his full mask and hat, and was dressed in blue jeans and a new western shirt he had never worn before. He looked out at the stadium and at the spots focused on that platform with the lone empty stool, and I thought he was going to be sick again. He squeezed my hand so tight it hurt. Finally Aben said, "It's time, kid. Break a leg!"

At that point a single spot hit right in front of the tunnel in which we were standing. The audience had their eyes on it, but they were still quiet. Then, over the loudspeaker system, a booming voice announced, "Ladies and gentlemen, Jetstream Records and Soldier Field are proud and pleased to present—"

Whatever was said after that we never heard. The audience let go with a spontaneous scream as if on cue, and the applause and whistling and yelling filled that stadium like roaring thunder.

"Go ahead, Spartacus," Aben said, as he gave Ronnie a slight nudge. "That's it . . . that's your cue."

Ronnie let go of my hand. It was numb from his squeezing it so tight. Then he looked at me, and said,

"See you later, buddy." With that he turned and faced toward the field . . . hesitated for just a moment . . . and stepped out into the spotlight.

CHAPTER

33

It was a long walk across the field to that stage, but Ronnie made it at a good, steady gait, the spot following him, the crowds screaming all the way. He climbed up the ten steps to the platform, took his place, and stood there facing the audience while the roar continued. Then the stage began to revolve. It was set on a huge turntable so that Ronnie didn't have to change positions to cover the whole arena. Each complete turn took about three minutes.

Ronnie didn't bow. He just picked up his guitar and kept standing there until he had slowly circled the whole audience. Then he held up one hand, and everyone quieted down, almost immediately. At that point he turned toward the group, beat off the tempo, and went into his first number.

I was so caught up in watching him that it was not until half the song was over that I realized I had planned to get to my seat for the concert. I ran through a passageway that Aben had shown me, got past a guard by showing my ticket, and arrived at my section just as Ronnie was finishing.

As I squeezed into place beside Darlene, she said, "Sam, where the heck have you been? I thought you'd never get here." Marsha gave me a "Hi"—she was with some long-haired, weird-looking kid—one of her punk friends.

"I know. I'm sorry," I said. There was so much screaming as Ronnie's song ended that we couldn't hear each other talk—which saved me from having to explain any further.

Darlene, Marsha, her friend, and I were in the front row. I couldn't complain about *these* seats! Next to me was Debbie, who gave me a grin when I came in. Next to her was Mrs. Finkelhof, then Mr. Finkelhof, and then Mr. Colter, who looked very uncomfortable. On the other side of our group was Ginny, and next to her, Andy Hamilton. All about us were Mapleton High School kids. I saw at least twenty faces I knew, and others I had seen around. The seating had been very carefully worked out. Wow, I thought. I'm not sure I want to be here when the shit hits the fan.

Ronnie started his second number without waiting for the audience to stop applauding, but they quieted down fast. He sounded fantastic. The amplifying system was the best, and Ronnie looked spectacular in those narrow spots pinned on him as he turned. The mask made it even more dramatic. He did song after song—all his record stuff, plus new ones that had been rehearsed for the third album, with no announcements in between. Just Spartacus and his music, and the audience loved it. They were quiet, and the sound balance was perfect, so that you could hear every word and note. Ronnie didn't go through a lot of gyrations like most performers, not even in the up-tempo numbers. He just stood there and played and sang those wonderful songs with his flawless phrasing. The concert came off in its own way like a true happening.

Finally, after being on for over an hour, Ronnie motioned for quiet once more, and then, for the first time that night, he spoke.

"Ladies and gentlemen, for my final number—"

There were screams of "No! No!"

" . . . I would like to do something new, a song that is perhaps very appropriate for tonight, titled, 'Will You Love Me Still.' "

I looked over at the Finkelhofs to see if they caught anything in the voice, but their faces were blank. Ronnie sounded different on that big sound system, and they didn't bat an eye.

Ronnie had never played that last song for me—he must have written it very recently. But whatever, it was a beauty, and knowing what he meant in every line, I got pretty choked up. The audience was completely quiet during the whole number, and even after it was over there was a delayed reaction before the screaming started again.

Ronnie bowed, just slightly, as the platform continued its slow three-hundred-and-sixty-degree turn. Then, when it came into position where Ronnie was directly facing our section of the stadium, it stopped. At that point he was also facing the television booth; it had all been carefully worked out. I glanced over at Mr. and Mrs. Finkelhof. Mr. Finkelhof was looking somewhat bored. He won't be bored long, I thought. Mrs. Finkelhof was applauding politely, and smiling down at Debbie, who was clapping with all her might. Mr. Colter was squirming, and looked like he wanted to leave. I glanced over at Ginny. Her face was flushed, and tears were running down her face. Andy didn't look too happy about her emotional reaction, but he was applauding just the same. The rest of the kids were screaming and yelling. Even Darlene and Marsha were caught up in it all. "He's fantastic, Sam," Marsha said. "He really is." You ought to know, I thought.

By now everyone was standing. Finally Ronnie held up his hands for silence, and the whole stadium went into a hush and sat down.

I knew the time had finally come.

CHAPTER

Ladies and gentlemen.

Ronnie began in a quiet, serious voice, speaking very slowly.

Thank you for your warm reception.

The audience started to applaud, but Ronnie gestured for quiet again.

As you know, it has been announced that I will unmask tonight, and show my face to the world for the first time since my most unusual success.

By now there was absolute silence in the stadium.

To most of you here, and to the television viewers

who are watching, I know this will be anticlimactic.
My face is just another face, and my name just another name—except, of course, to a select few who
are in this stadium tonight. I must tell you that at this
point in time, only four people know my true identity: first, of course, is Aben, the president of Jetstream Records; second, one member of my family;
third, my attorney; and fourth, a very close friend.
My own parents are totally unaware of the fact that
their son is Spartacus.

There was a gasp of surprise from the audience. I
looked over at Mr. and Mrs. Finkelhof, but there wasn't
a glimmer of suspicion in their eyes. Debbie had reached
over and was holding her mother's hand.

To Aben I want to say "thank you." His creative
business acumen had a great deal to do with my success. But much more than that, I thank him for his
always sound advice, and for allowing me to make
my own important decisions without undue pressure
or influence, even when those decisions were not necessarily in his own best interests.
To that one member of my family, I give my
thanks for her forbearance, under what must have
been most difficult circumstances. And I must add,
without her belief in me, all this might well never
have happened.
Now my attorney. In a strange way he had greater
problems with my secrecy than anyone. I must thank
him for his honesty, his commitment and respect for
the obligations of his profession, and for his diligence
on my behalf.
As for my very good friend, what can I say? Only
that I couldn't have made it without you, buddy. You
were the only one I could talk to—who understood
me in every respect. Without your companionship and
confidence, I would indeed have been lost.
Finally, my mother and father. I want to ask their

forgiveness. I ask them also to please try and understand. Perhaps there was some rebellion built into my
deception, particularly with my father. But there was
also fear. Whatever the reasons, now that this time has
come, I must tell them I wish I had done it another way.
Please, Mom and Dad, know that I love you both very
much. I will need your help and counsel now more than
ever. We have a great deal to talk about.

To all of you here tonight, some few of whom will
also know me, and to those watching on television, I
can only say that I have had many doubts about all that
has taken place. I wonder constantly if I have made the
right decision, the decision to openly live the life of that
"being" known only as Spartacus. For after tonight,
my life will undoubtedly never be the same. And whatever personal problems I faced in the past—and there
were many—I wonder what I face in the future.

I looked around. The audience was watching with rapt
attention. Ginny still had tears streaming down her face.
Debbie was hanging on to her mother's hand. Mrs. Finkelhof seemed caught up in the drama. Even Mr. Finkelhof appeared fascinated. Mr. Colter still looked like
he wanted to leave. Darlene was totally taken, and I must
tell you I had a hard time keeping dry eyes myself. Ronnie had made the moment very real. I guess that's because it came from the heart, and *was* very real.

You may have wondered why I selected Chicago
for this appearance. I had a reason . . . a reason very
personal to me, as you shall soon know. But for now
. . . well, I think there is little more I can say . . .
except that . . . the time has come.

Ronnie stood there for a moment. Finally he reached
up, took off his hat, hesitated, and then with one quick
motion pulled off his mask amid the flashing of cameras.

There was silence in the stadium for a full ten seconds. Then Ginny, staring straight ahead with a blank expression on her face, said out loud, "That's . . . that's . . . that's Ronnie Finkelhof!" There was another delayed reaction as Mrs. Finkelhof let out a piercing scream, and promptly fainted, while Mr. Finkelhof just sat there with his mouth hanging open. Ignoring his wife, he finally turned and gave a withering look to poor Mr. Colter. "I'm sorry, Ben," Colter said. "My hands were tied."

I looked at Darlene. She was also staring, with a numb expression on her face. Then Marsha turned to me. "My God, Sam," she blurted out, "I . . . I've had Spartacus!" That's the first time I knew Ronnie had made it that night! Her punk friend just let out a confused, "Hey, wot's happenin'?"

A kid behind me piped up, "Who is it?" Another answered, "Beats me." Then the word began to get around the Mapleton section that it was Ronnie Finkelhof. To many of them it had to be explained that he was "a kid in our school." Gradually the excitement of that news began to spread to students from other nearby areas, and the applause started. Then cheers, and finally the whole stadium stood up and began to applaud and scream, although most of them really didn't know why.

At that point the turntable started to revolve again, and as it did so, Ronnie and the group broke into "I'm Gonna Romance the Pants Off of You." At the sound of his original big hit, the screams and cheers exploded louder than ever. Ronnie, performing unmasked for the first time in his life, continued the encore as the platform circled, finally returning him to his original position facing the TV booth, where it stopped just as the song was ending.

While the screaming continued, Ronnie bowed,

waited, bowed again, and then turned and left the stage to go down the steps to the ground. Without looking back, he walked the length of the field and into the tunnel leading to the dressing rooms, a lone spotlight following him all the way. The applause continued long after he had disappeared from sight.

By now Mr. Finkelhof was attending to his wife, who seemed to be coming to—with Debbie helping. Ginny was staring straight ahead in a strange way. I wanted to get out of there, and asked Darlene if she would please excuse me. She just looked at me with her mouth open, speechless. "I've got to get back to Ronnie," I said, and took off without waiting for an answer.

But I never made it. Back at the entrance to the dressing room there were now three cops. One of them had let me out, but they refused to let me back in. I hadn't thought about that problem. I knew the Brinks truck was waiting down at the entrance to the field, but that was impossible as well. No way could I get through. I was just another fan to the police, no matter what I said! Aben hadn't figured that out, and I was screwed again!

Finally I decided it was hopeless, gave up, and went back to see if I could find Darlene and Marsha. But they were gone. So were the Finkelhofs.

I returned home on the bus alone, angry at Aben, annoyed with Ronnie, although I knew for no good reason, and disgusted with myself.

CHAPTER

35

I didn't see Ronnie that night, and the next day I figured I'd leave him alone with his parents. The morning paper had his picture on the front page, taken just as he pulled off his mask. SPARTACUS IS LOCAL BOY it said. On the inside was a picture of Mr. Finkelhof leaning over his wife trying to revive her, with Debbie helping. It was a funny scene, but I don't imagine the Finkelhofs thought so. I walked past their house during the afternoon, and there were a bunch of Mapleton High kids hanging around outside. I was suddenly very popular. They all wanted to talk to me, but I made excuses and got out of there. They were the same ones who twenty-four hours ago wouldn't have given me the time of day.

The news that night on television carried Ronnie's speech at the concert—the whole thing. I think people were touched by it. Then the following morning Ronnie called.

"How'd it go?" I asked.

"We were up all night after the concert, Sam. Yesterday was bad, too. Why don't you come on over?"

This time in front of Ronnie's house there was a mob of kids, mostly strange faces. There were also reporters and cameramen. Local cops were having a hard time keeping everyone off the property, but Debbie was at the door watching for me and waved me through. A couple of the cameramen took my picture.

"Ronnie's in his room, Sam," Debbie said. She looked tired. "Why don't you go right on up." Debbie seemed more mature somehow. I guess the whole experience had affected her as much as anyone.

Ronnie was sitting at his desk, just kind of staring. "Hi," he said. He looked beat.

"Was it rough?" I asked.

"Yeah, it was rough." Ronnie seemed in a daze.

"Well . . . ?" I had to know the details.

"Well, my folks were waiting when Aben dropped me home after the concert. He offered to come in with me, but I said this was something I had to face myself. When I got in the house, my mom gave me a big hug, but then she started to cry. Dad just sat in his chair. He didn't say a word, but I could see how angry he was. Finally, he opened up and let me have it."

"Bad, huh?"

"It was mostly about how I had made *him* look, and what would people think about a father that didn't have the confidence of his own son, and how ridiculous *he* would feel at the office, and what about *his* friends and neighbors, and how could I do this to *him*. Not once did he ask me what *I* had been through, or how *I* felt.

"When he finally settled down, I told him my plans, and that I wasn't going to Harvard in the fall. That did it! He wouldn't even talk to me after that. Sam, what can I do?" Ronnie was very down.

"It's a bummer, I know."

"We just can't communicate. If he only knew how much I need a father right now. I'm not up to all this stuff that's going on."

"Sorry, buddy. Wish I could help."

"You *do* help, Sam. Who else do I have to talk to?"

"What's Aben up to?" I asked. I wanted to get him off his old man.

"He wants me to have a personal manager—there's so much to handle—a CBS special, some kind of picture offer, the press. And Aben wants me to set up a road tour—worldwide. That reminds me, I've got to talk to you."

"What about?"

"I told you I want you with me, and I talked to Aben about it. I thought maybe you could be my road manager."

"Road manager?" I didn't know quite what that meant.

"It's an important job, handling all the logistics and setting up the facilities. You could do it great, and you know I'd pay you real well. What do you say, Sam?"

I had a funny reaction, although I didn't quite know for sure what it was. I was pleased that Ronnie followed through on what he had said to me before, but at the same time I had a sinking sensation in the pit of my stomach.

"Thanks, Ronnie," I said. "Let me think about it, huh?"

"Sure, Sam. I didn't mean to throw it at you so fast. But let me know. You understand how I feel . . ."

"I will. Just give me a couple of days to get my own head straight."

"Before I forget . . . Aben wants you to call."

"What's up?"

"I don't know, but he said he'd be in his office all day."

I didn't stay at Ronnie's much longer. He really looked

tired, and I knew his parents were both home. Mr. Finkelhof probably didn't want to face his office just yet, or
deal with the crowd and reporters waiting outside. I noticed, too, the phone was off the hook.

I called Aben and got through to him right away.
"Want to see you," he said. "Can you come in this
afternoon?" I said sure, and got there about 5:00 P.M.

"Sam, I want to have a very serious talk with you,"
Aben started out.

"Okay, Aben." I couldn't imagine what was coming.

"First of all, I want to talk about Ronnie. I don't know
if he told you or not, but he asked me to be his partner,
to handle all his affairs as a manager. He offered me a
half-interest in Spartacus."

"Are you going to do it?"

"No. I turned him down."

"Why? You've pretty much been doing it all along."

"That was different. Up to this point it was kind of
like *I* was Spartacus. But that's over. Ronnie is Spartacus
now. And that's as it should be. Much as I love Ronnie,
and I really do, it's not my bag to tie myself to any one
piece of talent. It takes an agent type, and even *they*
eventually look for a way out. That's why so many of
them end up producing, or even running a studio. Besides, I can't leave Jetstream to others. It's my baby, and
with all its problems, I still love the record business."

"Why are you telling me this, Aben? What's it got to
do with me?"

"I'm telling you because you have to make a decision,
too, Sam. Did Ronnie tell you he wanted you to be his
road manager?"

"Yes."

"You know Ronnie would be very generous."

"Yes, he said so."

"You also should know that as you got more into the business, you might be able to move up to more responsibility."

"I suppose so."

"Well, I've asked you to come here so that I could advise you not to accept."

"You kidding me, Aben?"

"I'm dead serious."

"Why? Where could I find a job like that? All I've had is a high school education. I don't get it."

"Sam, unless you're the star, that life stinks. You'd be on the road working your ass off, dealing with all kinds of details, and worse. The 'worse' is dealing with your bread and butter's emotions and temperament, and catering to his very often ridiculous needs and demands."

"But Aben, we're talking about Ronnie, not some crazy—"

"Ronnie, schmonnie," Aben interrupted. "I love him just as much as you do, but when that terrible pressure's on, they all come out pretty much the same."

I was flabbergasted at what Aben was saying. "What do you want me to do with my life, Aben? Shine shoes?"

"Come on, Sam. Hear me out. If all you needed was a job, I'd give you one right here at Jetstream. You're a bright kid, and your head's screwed on straight."

"Are you offering me a job, Aben?"

"No."

"Then what the hell are you getting at?"

"I want you to go to college. It's a tough world out there, Sam. And you're black. Which makes it even tougher. I want you to get an education before you do anything with your life."

"Brilliant idea, Aben. And how do I manage that? My

grades are okay, but not good enough to get me a scholarship.''

''It's all taken care of. All you have to do is say the word, and a trust will be set up to take you as far as you want to go. Colter will handle it—I've already talked to him.''

I was flabbergasted, and just sat there like a dummy. Finally I found my voice. ''Why, Aben? Why are you doing this?''

''Why? Let's just say it's the *least* I can do. I've built a fortune on Ronnie, Sam, and without you he might never have made it.''

''Is Ronnie in on this?'' I asked.

''You know he would be if I needed him. He just didn't think of it. He only thought of having you with him. Anyway, this is something I want to do myself.''

''What about Ronnie? He says he needs me.''

''Don't worry about Ronnie. Think of yourself for a change. He'll be okay. He's got to make it alone now, and he'll have plenty of professional support. After you graduate from college, I'm sure Ronnie will be there for you, if that's what you want.''

I don't know why, but I started to cry. I couldn't help myself. Too much was happening all at once. Between Aben and Ronnie I was overwhelmed. Aben laughed, came around the desk, and put his arm around me.

''I don't know what's the matter with me, Aben.'' I could hardly talk. ''I don't know what to say.''

''Don't say anything, Sam. Go home and talk it over with your folks. And please, don't thank me. I get embarrassed. If you make the decision—the right decision— just go see Colter. He'll take care of everything.''

I felt ashamed of myself for having misjudged Aben

so many times in the past, and rode home on the bus in a stupor.

CHAPTER

36

I did not discuss that conversation with Ronnie or anyone. I wanted to think about things by myself for a while. In the meantime, Aben was off lining up Ronnie's management staff, and Ronnie and I were able to spend some time together at his house. Also, Ronnie had had a call from Ginny, and that was something he wanted to talk about.

"What did she say?" I asked.

"You won't believe this, Sam. She wants to see me. You know what she said? She said, 'You know I always liked you, Ronnie.'"

"You going to see her?"

"Why not? She says her folks are out of town, and why don't I come over to her house tonight."

"Why don't you brush her off? She's done it to you often enough."

"I know. I thought of that, Sam. But I can't. I've still got this thing for her, dumb as it may be."

"Then get it out of your system," I said.

Ronnie slipped out the back door after dark and managed to make it to her house without being seen. The next day I didn't wait to call. I just came by to hear the news.

"She had on a silk blouse," Ronnie told me. "And one of those miniskirts. Funny thing was I really wanted her to be in her T-shirt and those tight blue jeans."

"Did you make it?" I asked. I couldn't wait for the details.

"Yes and no."

"What do you mean, for Christ's sake?"

"Well, at first it was pretty exciting. She practically threw herself at me. We were all over each other—grabbing, feeling—you know."

"Then you made it!"

"Wait, Sam. In the middle of everything she started calling me Spartacus, and telling me how much she loved me. She wasn't about to go to bed with *me*, Ronnie Finkelhof—she was making love to a dream."

"But didn't you want to go through with it anyway? It was still Ginny."

"I guess I might have, but then when the time came, she said, 'Take it easy with me, Spartacus. You're the first. You're the one I've been saving myself for.' "

"Wow."

"I couldn't do it, Sam. She turned me off. Ginny was about to sleep with Spartacus, not me. It was all in her stupid head. I lost all desire, and I also started to sag, if you know what I mean."

"What did you do?"

"I got up from the couch, started to put myself together, and told her I'd better go."

"You're kidding."

"I'm not. I tried to be as kind as I could, but she went bananas. First she started to cry. Then she started to beg. 'Please, Spartacus,' she said. 'Please. You're what I've dreamed of for so long. Don't leave me. Please, Spartacus.'

"I didn't know what to do. I tried to quiet her down, but nothing worked. Suddenly she jumped up, straightened her skirt, and buttoned up her blouse. Her face was red from crying, and she just stood there staring at me. Just staring, like she was trying to figure out who I was. 'Ronnie Finkelhof!' she finally said, like it was some kind of surprise. And then, Sam, you know what she did? She started to scream at me. 'Ronnie Finkelhof, you pig,' she yelled. 'What are you doing here? I hate you. I've always hated you. You are a no-good lousy ugly creep. Get out! Get out of my house this minute! And don't you ever come back.' ''

"Holy cow," was all I could say.

"That got me out of there in a hurry. And it's just as well, Sam. I guess I always knew that's the way it was. If I had played my cards right, I probably could have— or rather Spartacus could have had Ginny all the way. But I just didn't want her anymore. And when she let go at me, she made it very easy. I really should thank her for that.''

"I'll be damned," I said. "I guess that's the end of Ginny.''

"Yes, Sam," Ronnie said, "you can be sure. That's the end of Ginny.''

"Good.''

"But Sam . . .''

"Yes . . . ?''

"It's all there.''

"What's all there?''

"Her body. It's just like I imagined it would be. Too bad it has an empty head on top.''

I looked at Ronnie. He had a big grin on his face as he leaned back in his chair.

Yes indeed, he had come a long way.

CHAPTER

37

A week went by, and I had to make a decision.

Ronnie had made his choice, and now I had to make mine. First I had a long talk with my folks. I must admit the idea of going on the road with Ronnie was appealing. At the same time, I had had a small taste of being around the action without really being a part of it. So I listened to the older heads, and decided to accept Aben's offer.

Ronnie was disappointed, but he understood. He made a big thing about helping with the trust, but Aben wouldn't let him. "This is something I want to do all by myself," Aben said. "It makes me feel good."

What was left of the summer went very fast, and I didn't see too much more of Ronnie. Once the personal manager and talent agency from New York were set, they were all over him. There were plans to be made, musicians to hire, all kinds of publicity stuff like pictures, magazine interviews, tapings for talk shows, and all that. I hung out with Ronnie occasionally while all this was going on, but I felt in the way. There were always a lot

of people around him, and it was clear they had no use
for me.

Mr. and Mrs. Finkelhof did not interfere with Ronnie's activities. After all, he was eighteen now. Besides,
what could they do? His mom worried over him a lot,
but his dad just paid no attention after that first day. He
did not totally ignore Ronnie—he just didn't discuss anything with him, or acknowledge what was going on. He
acted like nothing was different, and went about his business. I think it was the cruelest kind of treatment.

Debbie was very subdued. Instead of glorying in her
brother's fame as she had always dreamed, she pulled
back, and went out in public only when she had to.
Maybe she felt guilty for what, at the time, had seemed
like an innocent prank. This was not the way she had
envisioned things, I'm sure.

Whatever they were all feeling, it was an uptight
household. I was sorry for them, even, in a funny way,
for Ronnie's dad. With all his lack of understanding, it
was still like he had lost a son. And I guess he had.

Of course, my own life was due for a big change, and
I had to make plans. I went to see Mr. Colter, and he
couldn't have been nicer. Aben had set it up just like he
said he would, and Colter had everything organized. With
his help I got into the Wharton School at the University
of Pennsylvania in Philadelphia. It was his alma mater,
and he said it was the best undergraduate business school
in the country, and the kind of education I should have.
I was due to leave in a few short weeks.

Ronnie's house got to be bedlam. There were people
all over the place, not to mention the mobs of kids outside that still came to gawk. Mr. Finkelhof was not very
tolerant of the inconvenience, so Ronnie finally made the
big move—the one that had to come sooner or later. He

packed up his things and took an apartment in New York. He had a lot to do there by now, what with getting ready to go on tour, and his agents needed him in the city. I don't think he was emotionally ready to leave home, but there wasn't much choice. As Aben said, Ronnie couldn't turn back now. No way. Right or wrong, good or bad, he was Spartacus, and nothing could change that.

"We'll keep in close touch, Sam," Ronnie said when I came over to say good-bye. "And we'll be together again before you know it."

"Sure we will, Ronnie. How are your folks taking your moving out?" I asked.

"My mom cried some. So did Debbie."

"Your dad . . . ?"

"He shook my hand, and wished me luck. Then he surprised me. 'I'm sorry, Ronnie,' he said. 'I guess I should have tried to understand better what was going on with you.' Then all of a sudden he choked up, and turned away. I put my arms around him and gave him a hug. That one moment is the closest we've ever been. I felt a lot better about leaving after that."

"I'm glad, Ronnie."

"Now don't forget. We've got to keep in touch."

"Sure Ronnie. You bet we will." But as I said it, somehow I knew we were both talking through our hats, and that this was really good-bye.

Ronnie called me a couple of times from New York, but even on the phone I could hear how busy he was. Anyway, by then it was time for me to get on the plane for Philadelphia, and in the third week of September I entered the freshman class of the University of Pennsylvania.

It was exactly two years to the day that I had first met Ronnie Finkelhof.

CHAPTER

38

Well, the rest is pretty much history. That speech Ronnie made at the big concert had reached maybe seventy million people watching on television, not counting those who saw it repeated on the news. It was printed in the entertainment sections of newspapers, in fan magazines—even *Time* and *Newsweek* carried it. It seemed to have touched everyone, and the whole event had appealed to a very broad audience.

Ronnie's career continued to blossom. I followed it closely in the papers, and never missed him when he was on television. I got phone calls from him occasionally, but I was never in my dorm, and then couldn't get through when I tried to call him back. I also got a card from Hollywood, but after a while I stopped hearing from him. I understood. He must have been very busy.

After my freshman year at Penn, I went home for the summer, and got a job clerking in the office of a brokerage firm. I was a college student now—no more supermarket for me. It kept me busy, and it was good to see my folks. But Ronnie's ghost was everywhere. It was lonesome. Some of the kids from Mapleton High were a little more friendly, but I really didn't want any part of them.

I did stop in to say hello to the Finkelhofs one evening.

They were glad to see me, and we talked a lot about Ronnie. He had been calling home about once every couple of weeks, but they were anxious to know what I heard and what I knew, which wasn't much. Later Debbie pulled me aside.

"Sam, did Ronnie ever tell you about his taking my diary?"

"Sure, he told me. But he never looked inside."

"I know that," Debbie said. "Now I want you to read it."

"You want *me* to read it?" I wasn't sure I had heard right.

"You're his best friend. Maybe some day, when the time is right, you'll tell him about it. I know he must have had a lot of terrible ideas about what was in there." Debbie had turned her diary to an entry going back before any of the Spartacus stuff had happened. We sat in Ronnie's room while I read.

Dear Diary,
    Today at Phillips Drugstore an awful thing happened. I was sitting in a booth by myself having a milkshake when I heard some older kids in the booth behind me talking about Ronnie. They didn't know I was there. It was a boy and a girl. The boy called her Ginny, and he kept saying how he thought Finkelhof had the hots for her and how he was staring at her all the time. Then they would both laugh, and the boy said she should go out with him and put him out of his misery. And the girl said she'd rather go out with Frankenstein, and they laughed some more. They talked about what a goon he is, and I felt just terrible. I couldn't finish my milkshake. I felt like telling them off and that my brother is the smartest and nicest boy I know and better than both of them put together. But I just ran out of there and didn't say a word. I don't know

what I should have done. I feel very bad and don't
want Ronnie ever to know about this.

When I finished, I looked up at Debbie. Her eyes were
wet.

"I don't think that would bother him much now," she
said. "And I wanted you to know, too."

I looked at little Debbie with new respect. This was
quite a young lady. I leaned over and gave her a kiss on
the cheek. "You're okay," I said. "I don't think Ronnie
gave too much thought about what was in your diary,
Debbie, but I think he ought to know what kind of a
super kid sister he has." I left her sitting alone in Ronnie's room.

My next year at Penn was a little easier for me than
the first, and I was getting into my studies more. Ronnie
and I were pretty much out of touch by this time, but in
my junior year Spartacus made an appearance in Philadelphia. A week before his concert I got a ticket in the
mail, and a note.

Dear Sam,
    I had Philly booked special. Miss you. Please come
and meet me backstage after the concert. Have to
catch a plane that night, but we can have a little time.

                              Spartacus (Ronnie to you, buddy)

Of course, I went to the concert, and had a seat right
down front. I knew from television, and pictures I had
seen of Ronnie, that he had changed his act a lot, but I
guess I wasn't prepared for what came out on that stage.
Ronnie—I can't even call him that—Spartacus was
dressed in a Roman gladiator outfit. He had a metal
breastplate, arm bands, thongs on his feet, the whole bit.

That Aben! It was what he had in mind from the start. That was to be Ronnie's gimmick, and why he gave him a name neither of us understood at the time.

The opening number was pure hard rock. Ronnie's beautiful guitar was now replaced with an electric model that he swung around like a baton while he played. He had let his hair grow long, and he tossed it about with every move. And he moved a lot. I guess you'd say he was dancing, if you want to call it that. I have to say it was a shock. But he was good. Damn good!

After the concert I pushed my way through to the stage door, and went inside. There was a big bruiser of a man standing there with his legs apart, guarding the entrance.

"What do you want, kid?" he said.

"I'd like to see Ro—uh, Spartacus."

"Spartacus don't see nobody after a concert."

"Look, mister, I'm sure he'll see me. Would you please tell him Sam is here."

"Oh, yeah, Sam. . . . he's expectin' you." The big gorilla stepped aside to let me through.

"Sam!!!" It was Ronnie down the hall, standing in front of his dressing room. "Sam, get your ass down here!"

I would hardly have known Ronnie, even up close. He had his costume off, and was in a white terry-cloth robe. He was all sweaty, and his long hair was sticking to his face and neck. He wasn't wearing glasses—he must have had on contacts. Anyway, he grabbed me and gave me a big hug.

"Goddamn, it's good to see you!" Ronnie said as we went into his dressing room.

"It's good to see you, too, Ronnie." I felt a little awkward, but Ronnie was all smiles and very much at ease.

"It's funny being called Ronnie. Guys around here call me Sparty."

"Okay, Sparty," I said. It sounded silly.

Just then some kid stuck his head in the door of the dressing room. "You'd better get dressed, Spart. You only have five minutes."

"Okay, Pete, let them wait. Got to talk to my friend."

"Who was that?" I asked.

"My road manager—he's always after me about something!" (There but for the grace of God . . . I thought.) Ronnie looked at me for a minute. "It's been too long," he said.

"I know. We've both been working hard. How are you? How's your family? Everybody okay?" I was beginning to feel more at home with my old friend.

"Yeah, they're fine. They all came to my concert in Detroit. Even Dad. Debbie tells me he brags a lot about his famous son."

"I'm glad."

"They ask about you all the time. You graduate next year, right?"

"Looks like it will be summa cum laude. Would you believe it?"

"Why not? Congratulations! I could *use* a good college man. What do you say?"

Before I could answer, the dressing room door opened again and Pete stuck in his head. "Spart—"

"Okay, in a few minutes."

I knew Ronnie's time was tight, and decided I'd better let him know my plans now. "I've had early acceptance at Harvard Law School," I said.

Ronnie looked at me in surprise. Then he broke into a big smile. "That's fantastic!"

"I'm gonna go."

"Of course—of course you're gonna go. Can I help?"

"Thanks, Ron, but Aben's got it set up all the way."

We were both quiet for a minute, but I could see that Ronnie was genuinely pleased for me. "Study hard, buddy," he finally said. "I'm gonna need a good lawyer more than anything else around here. Y'know, Sam, you made the right decision when you went to college."

I wondered then what Ronnie was thinking, and decided to ask him point-blank. "What about you, Ron? Did *you* make the right decision?"

Before he could answer, Pete came bursting in again. "Spart—for Christ's sake—"

"Okay, okay—in just a few minutes!"

When Pete left, Ronnie explained to me what that was all about. "I always go back onstage and do encores, but I make them wait for a while, as if the concert's over. Then I do kind of an aftershow. It's part of the game, and they know it."

"Oh, I'm sorry, Ron," I said. "You go ahead."

"No, not yet. You asked me a question."

"You don't have to answer it."

"But I want to. I've thought about it many times."

Ronnie was quiet for a moment, and he seemed a little like the old Ronnie Finkelhof. Finally he looked straight at me. "Sam," he said, "being a star is being wanted . . . being envied . . . being *loved*. Think back to what I *used* to be. I'm king of the hill now. But it's more than that cheering audience out there. It goes further. You know, we all feel inadequate, inferior, at one time or another. Left out. No matter who we are. But when you're a star, you don't have to face that. I have access to the world. My opinions are printed on every subject from politics to marriage. Every move I make is given significance—whether or not there is any. I've even been invited to the White House! I'm *somebody* now, Sam.''

Ronnie paused and looked thoughtful. Then he went on. ''There's a price to pay, sure. Sometimes I yearn just to be left alone. But it's all worth it. I have no regrets. None. I love being Spartacus. I don't care if it's a long life or a short one. It's a kick in the ass, like nothing I could have imagined.''

I looked at Ronnie carefully. I knew he meant it. ''I'm glad, Ron,'' I said.

Just then Pete came back. ''Spart, c'mon, man! They're tearing the roof off out there!''

''Go ahead, Ron. I've got to get back to the campus anyway.'' I figured I should get out of his way.

''No, don't go. Stay and watch. Please. Pete, take my friend back in the wings . . . Okay, Sam?''

''Sure, Ron,'' I said. ''You're the boss.''

As Pete and I left the dressing room, a cute-looking girl brushed past me on the way in. She was blond, blue-eyed, and looked a lot like Ginny. And she was wearing blue jeans—very tight ones. As I watched through the open door, I saw her give Ronnie a big kiss, and then hold his robe as he took it off. I couldn't help but smile.

The audience was screaming as Pete and I went into the wings, and when Ronnie came on, they really exploded. Ronnie was not wearing his costume—just blue jeans and a shirt. No gimmicks now, no Spartacus, just plain old Ronnie Finkelhof. The audience went crazy. Finally Ronnie got them quieted down and spoke into the mike.

''Tonight is very special for me,'' Ronnie started out. ''There's an old friend of mine backstage, and I want to do a song I wrote a long time ago. I've been saving it for the right occasion, and I think this is it. It's in memory of my days behind the mask, and in dedication to the one who was so much a part of my life, who shared those times with me.'' Then Ronnie looked over at me and said:

"This is for you, Sam."

The song he sang for the first time that night has since been recorded. It wasn't his biggest hit, but it sure was for me. I'll never forget the lyrics.

> The world often seemed so wrong,
> Made me wonder did I belong,
> Met a friend and I understood,
> That I belonged and always would;
> We're one and the same,
> Both there for the world to blame;
> Ooooohhhhh . . . my friend and I.
>
> The life of a lonely heart,
> A beam of light in a world of dark,
> Given hope from one who cares,
> Strength to smile at the empty stares,
> We're one and the same,
> Tryin' to win in a losing game,
> Ooooohhhhh . . . my friend and I.
>
> All the times that helped us grow,
> Toward a life we did not yet know,
> And when it all has been said and done,
> Please remember you're still the one,
> We're one and the same,
> Only different by color and name,
> Ooooohhhhh . . . my friend and I.*

By the time he finished I was pretty misty. The audience loved it, and were screaming and carrying on. I knew Ronnie had to rush for a plane after the concert, and I hate good-byes anyway, so I decided it was time

---

Song "My Friend and I," words and music by Christopher Alan Livingston © 1985.

to leave. Ronnie was just standing there smiling, looking off at me in the wings while the audience went crazy. I gave him a wave, and he gave me a salute, and I turned and walked back through the wings, out the stage door, and into the Philadelphia night. I knew Ronnie and I would be together again before too long, but only after we did what we both had to do.

It had rained while I was in the theater, and as I walked down the wet street on my way back to the campus, I thought about a lot of things. I thought about how times have changed. When I watch the late show on television, I see macho guys with square jaws and rugged good looks—and names like Clark Gable or Gary Cooper. Then a whole generation went for guys with makeup on their faces, or with girl's names, or punk, or gimmicks of one kind or another. But it's what's behind and underneath it all that counts. It's talent. That's what made it possible for Ronnie Finkelhof to take off his mask and still be Spartacus to his fans. He never lost one. Ronnie Finkelhof, Superstar!

As for me, I was grateful for the way things were turning out. Me, Sam Bennett . . . Esquire! I never would have believed it possible. It's there for everyone, I guess. We *all* have a crack at it . . . at changing . . . at growing into whatever we want to be—if we want it badly enough. We *can* leave the old behind. Like Ronnie. You might say Ronnie Finkelhof is dead.

Long live Spartacus!

Long live the Spartacus in all of us!

Young Adults In the SP●TLIGHT

from
JUNIPER BOOKS